The
IRON

Introduction to *The Iron Veil*

I have always been haunted by Berlin, where much of the action of this book takes place, ever since I was posted there as a young National Service Intelligence Corps Officer in the winter of 1957. Believe it or not, that was several years *before* the Berlin Wall was built; it finally happened in 1961. At that time, the division between the Russian sector and the French, American and British sectors was delineated by a barbed wire fence. We British officers were allowed to pass freely into the Russian sector and, on one memorable occasion, I remember returning home after a night at the Stadt's Opera in East Berlin – the seats were very cheap there – reporting to my Commanding Officer that "they seem to be building some sort of wall around the Brandenburg Gate". A great story and a true one.

I have just been back to Berlin after an absence of almost forty-five years, and what changes have taken place. The new Berlin is a vibrant, bustling building site, and the trees in the *Tiergarten* have grown tall. When I was there as a soldier not a tree existed; everything had been cut down for firewood in the bleak post-war years.

Berlin, then and now, was a haunting place full of excitement, contrasting lifestyles, and touches of decadence. It is a wise city, a courageous city and a perverse city at the same time. Back in 1971, when I wrote this book, which was then entitled *Sonntag*, I was a diplomat serving in the British Embassy in Bonn. Reading it again now, I am pleased by the way it has stood the test of time. The mood still holds: the overhang of good and evil in its history is still present in Berlin as we enter this new millennium.

For the record, *Sonntag* sold well, and was translated into eight or nine different languages.

The
IRON VEIL

Michael Shea

severn House

This title first published in Great Britain 2000 by
SEVERN HOUSE PUBLISHERS LTD of
9–15 High Street, Sutton, Surrey SM1 1DF.
Originally published 1971 as *Sonntag*, under
the pseudonym *Michael Sinclair*.
This title first published in the U.S.A. 2000 by
SEVERN HOUSE PUBLISHERS INC of
595 Madison Avenue, New York, N.Y. 10022.

British Library Cataloguing in Publication Data
Shea, Michael, 1938-
   The iron veil
   1. Suspense fiction
   I. Title
   823.9'14 [F]

   ISBN 0-7278-5465-8

For my wife

All situations in this publication are fictitious and
any resemblance to living persons is purely coincidental.

Printed and bound in Great Britain by
MPG Books Ltd, Bodmin, Cornwall.

ONE

Marienborn, Friday Morning

Scholz leant forward over the steering-wheel and clicked down the wiper switch below the dashboard. Sleet was driving thickly against the windscreen now, but inside the cab of the lorry it was almost too warm with the heat from the engine. He stretched slightly in his seat and blinked, adjusting his eyes to the glare of the headlights catching the falling flakes.

In a few moments the lights of the Marienborn Checkpoint would be visible ahead. Then, unless the border guards were feeling kinder than usual, there would be the long wait while papers were checked and he would certainly be late home for breakfast. He was still angry with the men at the loading-bay for having caused him such a late start from Charlottenburg.

He drove carefully. It would be idiotic to make up lost time by breaking the rigorously enforced speed limit and have the zonal police take him in for questioning. Not that it was likely unless they were looking for an opportunity to create an incident. He had nothing to hide. A straightforward consignment of refrigerators from Berlin, bound for the free markets of Western Europe.

Ahead were the arc-lights, and, to the right and left, the beacons from the stilted sentry towers where the *Vopos*—the People's Police—would be watching the

Curtain with its tall electric fences, mined strips and barbed wire. He cautiously pulled into the lorry-park beside the first red and white barrier, switched off his engine and lights, and, taking his papers from the rack, opened the door of the cab and jumped out into the cold.

Inside the wooden hut which housed the border control óffice it was thick with the smell of cheap cigars. Scholz wordlessly pushed his papers over the counter towards the sleepy-looking soldier. The man motioned him to wait on one of the plain wooden benches which lined the walls.

Thank God. At least there were no other vehicles waiting for clearance at that time of night, and he didn't have to queue. He lit a cigarette, and pulling a crumpled copy of *Bild Zeitung* out of his pocket relaxed as well as he could on the hard seat.

Through a glass partition behind the counter, he could see two Russian soldiers with dark red bands on their peaked caps. They were standing with their greatcoats still on beside a round cast-iron stove. Obviously they had just been relieved at the barriers, and their broad Mongolian faces were relaxed and happy. To their right, hanging on the wall, was the stereotyped picture of Lenin in a simple wooden frame.

A soldier in East German uniform came in and sat down on the bench beside Scholz, rubbing his hands.

"Guten Morgen. Kalt!" The soldier was friendly. It certainly was cold. Outside, the sleet had turned to snow.

"Ja." Scholz acknowledged the remark cautiously. He had always felt that the less he said to people while

he was travelling through the Zone, the better. "Much traffic tonight?" he asked uninterestedly, but attempting to be polite.

"Very little . . . the Capitalists can't stand the cold." The soldier laughed. "Only two vehicles, Mercedes both of them, since midnight. You're late, aren't you?"

"Got held up loading in Berlin."

"Never mind. You'll be on your way soon. At least you don't have to stand out in the cold like me." The soldier nodded briefly to his colleague behind the counter, and went out again into the night.

Scholz turned back to his *Bild Zeitung*. It would be very late now before he got home to his flat on the outskirts of Essen. His wife was expecting him home for breakfast. But she would understand that as it was nearly two-thirty in the morning, it would be better to pull into a parking-lot after he was across the border and sleep till dawn. Besides, if the snow settled, the auto-bahn surface would be dangerous. He was tired. He could sleep comfortably in the bunk behind the driving seat.

His thoughts were interrupted by the soldier calling him over to the counter.

"*Alles in Ordnung*—everything's correct. Please go out and clear your cargo through customs control."

Scholz took his papers, turned up the collar of his jacket, and went out into the snow. A customs officer appeared almost at once. He carried a torch and made a fairly brisk but superficial check of the load under the tarpaulins. But with a ruler and a wire rod he carefully examined the measurements of the lorry's huge diesel tank, both inside and out, looking for false compartments where people or things might be smuggled out of the Zone. It had happened before.

"O.K., you can go now."

Scholz climbed thankfully into the still warm cab, started the engine and drove slowly across the cobbles to the barrier. He waved his papers at the Russian soldier who raised the red and white striped pole to let him through. This procedure was repeated at a second barrier, where, for a moment, he was blinded by a searchlight from one of the guard-towers which swept the lorry two or three times, looking for any refugee, perhaps, who might be clinging to it.

Then along the strip of badly kept autobahn, through no-man's-land to the Helmstedt Checkpoint, the more friendly border guards and the red-capped British Military Police who manned the post on the Western side. No trouble there, and in a few moments he was through into the Federal Republic.

Shortly after passing the low-lying huts of the British N.A.A.F.I. buildings, almost hidden under their quickly thickening blanket of snow, he pulled into the first parking-place he could find, switched off the engine and prepared to settle down for the night. It was almost three-thirty.

As he was taking his boots off, through the snow which was rapidly obscuring the view through the windscreen, he saw a man running towards him across the parking area. He must have come from the Volkswagen van parked about fifty metres away, for this was the only other vehicle in sight.

The man shouted something to him, and with a scowl of annoyance Scholz wound down his window.

"What d'you want?" he asked brusquely.

"Can you give me a lift on to the Hanover turn-off? My van's broken down." He was a little man in blue overalls.

"Nothing doing. Sorry. I'm here for the night." Scholz began to wind up the window again.

"It's very urgent. I'll give you fifty marks."

"Nothing doing, I said. Too tired, and the roads are too bad with this snow."

"A hundred, then."

God, the man must really be desperate. That was three or four days' pay to a lorry driver. "What's the matter with your Volks? Can't you do anything with it?" Despite his tiredness he felt almost sorry for the little man.

"No, impossible," the man said hurriedly. In the snow, his face looked white and strained. "How about it?"

Scholz thought slowly. A hundred would come in handy. Bloody nuisance, though. At least an hour's drive to Hanover, but then he could bed down again if he felt like it.

"O.K. Get your stuff."

"I haven't anything I need take. I'm ready now." The man looked round almost nervously at the van behind him. The snow was falling very thickly now, and it was almost hidden where it stood up against the pine trees.

They drove through the night. The going was slow, and once or twice the great lorry skidded across the lanes of the autobahn. They hardly saw another vehicle.

"Come from Berlin?" Scholz asked.

"Yes . . . I suppose so. Potsdam really. Half an hour or so before you did."

Neither spoke again. Scholz wondered vaguely why the man lied to him. He remembered the soldier at the border saying that only two cars—Mercedes—had gone through since midnight. Still, a hundred marks was a hundred marks.

Funny little man he was. Nervous type. Scholz cast the occasional glance towards him. Blue boiler suit on. Bit too big for him. Seemed to have a white collar and a tie on underneath. Odd, but of course he would have put on overalls when he was trying to repair his van. Yet his hands were small, neat and clean, almost like a woman's.

Essen, Friday Evening

Scholz was wakened by his wife at about six in the evening. He had slept deeply for several hours. He remembered that shortly after dropping his passenger near Hanover, the snow had cleared so he had driven on till dawn, left the lorry at the depot, and come home on an early bus, to sleep through the day instead.

His wife carried a tray with some food. Schnitzel, potato salad, a beer and a copy of the evening paper.

"Thanks, love," he said as she went out again. Almost worth the drive, treatment like that, and a hundred marks into the bargain. He'd buy the wife something for herself as a surprise. That'd be nice.

He picked up the newspaper and began to eat. He

saw the banner headlines and the photographs. Two bodies found in a van near the frontier, by Helmstedt. Funny that: he'd been past there just that morning. He read slowly and with some effort as always. The bodies had been hacked about quite unrecognizably. One had been a woman's. Time of death, around midnight. Place of death, a parking area just off the autobahn.

Scholz remembered the bloodstains on the passenger's seat. He had seen them as he left the lorry in the depot at daylight. The night-watchman had asked him if he had cut himself. "No," he had said. "It must have been my passenger." He had forgotten all about it in his tiredness. It was quite a lot of blood, though.

Scholz carefully put the tray on one side, got up and dressed quickly. He was almost ready by the time his wife came in.

"You haven't eaten anything." She was surprised. "Are you all right? You look a bit pale."

"I have to go out," he said. "Don't worry, I'll be back soon."

TWO

Westminster, Monday Evening

The corridors were crowded. It was almost eleven, and the House had just risen. Members were collecting their coats and papers, making their way to taxis and tubes, or to the bars for a final quick drink before closing time.

A tall, heavily-built man, probably in his middle thirties, showed an orange pass to the policeman on duty at the St Stephen's Entrance, and then walked quickly past, along the tiled corridors and up some stairs, stopping at an anonymous oak door. He went in.

"Is the Minister back yet?" he asked the secretary who was sitting typing just inside the door.

"He's just gone in, Mr Armstrong. I told him you were coming. But he wants to get away soon. He's got an early start tomorrow, you know." She obviously wanted to get away too. There were too many late hours spent in the corridors of power.

He walked across the ante-room and through into the Minister's office. He didn't knock. Early on he had learned that knocking on doors was more disturbing than the occasional unwanted entrance.

The Minister was signing some letters at his desk. A lamp with a green shade cast a peculiarly cold light over the historic room. A Private Secretary hovered behind, feeding his chief with files. Neither of them paid any attention to his arrival.

Eventually the Private Secretary stole across the carpet to him. "Good evening, Mr Armstrong. Would you mind taking a seat for some minutes? It shouldn't take long," he whispered.

Armstrong sat on a long leather-covered settee. He pulled a flimsy piece of telegram paper from his inside pocket and refreshed his memory on some of the details of the case he had been instructed to report to the Minister. He wasn't particularly relishing the task. To report a complete failure was bad enough, but it was an operation which the Minister had only reluctantly agreed to in the first place, after a great deal of lobbying and persuasion, and then only on the understanding that it was simple and had a hundred per cent chance of success.

"Thank you, Richard. The rest can wait till I get back tomorrow night." The Minister handed his Private Secretary a bundle of papers.

"Would you like me to wait, Minister?"

"Not necessary, I think," said the Minister looking up. "Good evening, Armstrong, sorry to keep you. I don't think we need Richard, do we, nor Miss Simms next door?"

"No, Minister. It's a verbal account only. Nothing to be written down."

"Good night then, Minister. I've got all your papers and the despatch box. I'll take them back to Downing Street as I go. Good night, Mr Armstrong." The Private Secretary left the two men alone.

"Well, what's wrong?" The Minister with his hard northern accent was terse. "I imagine they wouldn't have sent you over at this time of night unless something was wrong."

"I'm afraid it's the 'Sonntag' operation, Minister. It's come unstuck, putting it mildly. We've lost two of our best people—one, a woman."

"What d'you mean lost? I knew this thing was half-baked. Have they been caught? If your bloody Director hadn't got at the P.M. behind my back, it wouldn't have reached the drafting stage, I can tell you." The Minister was working up to one of his much publicized rages.

Armstrong waited until he had subsided a little and then went on unemotionally: "They're dead, Sir. Found in a van just this side of the zonal border. Here's the report." He handed over a piece of paper which the Minister read in silence.

"Well that's the end of that. And someone is for the jump, I can tell you. Misinformed, that's what I was. If this gets out—God forbid—I'd have to resign."

"There is little danger of it being traced to us, Minister. I wouldn't worry. . . ."

"Wouldn't worry! Wouldn't worry! What the bloody hell d'you mean? Two people have died. Is it my fault or isn't it? Don't you tell me not to worry."

"It was their job, Minister." Armstrong remained almost unmoved.

"God, you people are cold. No human warmth in you. If I had my way, your whole bloody set-up would be wound up. It's not bloody wartime. What have the Germans said about it?"

"The Federal Government, Minister, were unfortunately not fully in the picture. Their security agency is now at least, er, partially aware of the circumstances, and they are acting wonderfully. The German press have it as the result of a jealous husband quarrel."

"Pretty violent quarrel, judging from the details. Now what?"

"Well, Minister, we . . . we haven't decided. You see we don't yet know how it happened or how they came to be in a van near the border. They should have been a hundred or so miles away. We're working under considerable difficulty."

"I know, I know. You can't go around questioning people like a village bobby. But here's one piece of news to take back with you. All action, and I mean all action, on this Sonntag thing is to stop forthwith, until you've cleared up the mess. Is that understood?"

"But, Sir, we've got things boiling on this on at least a dozen fronts. It will be very difficult, if not impossible to get messages to our people in the, er, field . . ."

"You heard. I'm sure you're efficient enough to have emergency procedures laid on for occasions like this."

"But, Minister, I have to say that such action may jeopardize the positions or even the lives of . . ."

"Don't 'But, Minister' me, Armstrong. Are you trying to threaten me by any chance? I won't stand for it!"

"No, Minister. I'll report what you've said immediately." Despite himself, Armstrong was shaken to silence by the violence of the man's reaction. Many years exposed to the immorality of politics had obviously still left the old politician bitter about intelligence operations in all their forms. He remembered the idealism of some of the minutes he had seen written in the Minister's shaky handwriting.

There was a long and unpleasant silence. The Minister, sitting in a pool of green light, was staring at the piece of paper he held in his hand.

Eventually, "Don't you realize, Armstrong," he said quietly, "that two people have died. D'you know what Ministerial responsibility is about, Armstrong? Do you? It's not just answering nasty questions on the floor of the House. It's something more, something inside you, Armstrong. Something in here." He stabbed a short, stubby finger towards his chest. "Don't you realize, Armstrong?"

"Will that be all, Minister?"

The Minister on an impulse swung forcefully round on his swivel chair towards the bookcases behind him. They contained leather-bound copies of Hansard. He nodded slowly and without looking up.

At the office Armstrong reported the result to the Night Duty Officer, and arranged for the Director himself to be told immediately. He didn't bother to take his coat off. There was nothing more to be done—or that he could do. He looked at his watch. The bar of the club would still be functioning.

Outside, he began to search for a taxi, then decided to walk. It would be good for his peace of mind after the storm of the interview, and even better for the beginnings of a spreading waist-line. Not that there was too much in his mind that needed pacifying. It had been unpleasant, but all in a day's work. He had only been the messenger-boy, and now it was over, thank God. His was Liaison Section. The follow-up was Security's pigeon.

When he thought about it at all, Armstrong shared a belief held strongly among certain Civil Servants that the good ones should possess a positive detachment from any personal involvement in the subject matter. In addition one had to have a precise awareness of the limits and boundaries of one's place in the machine. Personal involvement was untidy; empire building was dangerous. Emotions led to subjective value-judgements, just as poaching on others' preserves led to bitterness. What one needed to serve the State well was an ability to penetrate and weigh opposing, or apparently opposing, arguments dispassionately, and find a conclusion which was rational and didn't do too much violence to the facts. Good international relations weren't served by sympathy or charm, and least of all by—what was it the Minister had said? No matter. He dismissed the thing from his mind. Security would pick up the bits.

He walked quickly and began thinking of his waist-line: that morning it had been a near thing with the top trouser-button. And he spent time on his personal appearance, though sometimes a vague worry crept in that a wife would have noticed things that needed more than a laundry and a good tailor to rectify. The monasticism, the single-mindedness needed in his job, these he liked, but he mustn't go to seed physically . . . or mentally. What had that girl said to him a week or two ago after that disastrous dinner? He had attempted an affair and she had dismissed him. She hadn't quite said she found him boring, but had suggested he didn't treat her as a person, that he didn't talk to her except forced small-talk. Something about not communicating—all of it nonsense,

of course. Lucidity had been one of the terms used
in his praise in his latest personal report. He had seen it.
The girl had been a bit grim in any case; he could barely
remember her name. It *had* been worrying for a little
while, though.

He turned up St Martin's Lane and along to the right.
The porter was at the main door, looking up and down.
He smiled as he recognized Armstrong.

"Good evening, Sir. Telephone call for you. They said
you'd be arriving any moment now. They're on the
line now."

The D.O. was brief. "The Director asked me to get
hold of you. He wants you to take on this wind-up
business from now on. Security's under pressure it seems.
It's immediate action, I'm afraid, and there's some tidy-
ing-up action on hand more or less straight away. I think
you'd better look in again. . . ."

THREE

Islington, Tuesday Morning
The early morning mist was beginning to clear slowly, and out of the fourth floor window the North London roofs took on a new sharpness. A flight of starlings swooped and settled on the dirty brown Victorian clock-tower.

The girl stood at the kitchen sink by the window, washing breakfast dishes. The flat was quiet now that the children had left for school. She heard the postman trudge slowly down the common stairway. There was no rattle of the letter-box at the door. Once again, nothing. It was three weeks now. She would ring his office to see if anything had happened to him.

Her dark hair swept back and held behind her head in a loose bow showed up the anxiety in her face. Perhaps more handsome than good-looking, her features demonstrated strongly for a moment her half-Jewish background, the resoluteness of her émigré, middle-European father, and the poise of her English mother.

She paused almost absentmindedly and gazed out at the starlings, which, frightened by something unseen, were wheeling over the roof-tops once again. Aware of new footsteps on the stairway, heard clearly through the thin walls of the flat, she wondered vaguely who it could be. Too early for the milk, and it wasn't the day for the laundry-man. She picked up a cup and began washing it mechanically.

The doorbell shrilled and startled her. She dried her hands on her apron as she went through to the hall.

"Mrs Donovan?" The man looked almost too respectable for that part of London.

"I'm sorry. My sister's taken the children to school and then she was going shopping. She won't be back much before twelve."

"Then you are Miss Weinberg?"

"Yes," she replied, surprised that he should know her name. "Can I help you?"

"D'you think I could come in for a minute. It's you I wanted to see. I am afraid that I, er, have some bad news for you."

"It's Alex." Her reaction was automatic. The three weeks without a letter had conditioned her subconscious. "What's happened?" She stood aside as he came into the hall, shut the door behind him and then led him into the sitting-room.

"I'm from Alex's office. I'm a colleague. We just got the news yesterday and it took us a little time to find you. We didn't know that, er, you were engaged. My name is Armstrong."

"What's happened to him," she whispered, sitting down slowly on a couch. "Where is he?"

"I'm very much afraid that Alex—your fiancé—is dead, Miss Weinberg. May I say how sorry we all . . ."

"It can't be true." She sank back, cushioning the panic. After a few moments she asked: "What happened? . . . Oh, I'm . . . Do have a seat Mr . . ."

"Armstrong. I'm afraid he was killed, Miss Weinberg— in Germany." Armstrong was uncomfortable. Why had they made him take on a filthy job like this? Why always Armstrong, the bearer of bad tidings? He felt almost sorry for the girl. She looked bewildered rather than sad. She was also attractive. He had felt that the Minister's anger and contempt last night had been embarrassing enough. This certainly was worse and it wasn't finished. It was his pigeon now, too. He much preferred it when they were only names on a piece of paper.

Clumsily he tried to comfort her. "We're doing everything—all the arrangements, that is. He had no relations, had he?"

"He almost had me," she breathed. She suddenly seemed to summon up some energy and began to compose herself. "I'm so sorry. It's such a shock. I had thought something was wrong. Please tell me what happened."

"Perhaps you'd like to wait a bit, till you feel a little steadier." He tried to be kind and he wanted to escape. He could send someone else later.

"I'd like to know." It was final.

He reluctantly told her the story about the van near the Curtain, of the two bodies, of what the German press were saying. He stared at the wall in front of him as he spoke. It would have been impossible otherwise.

When he finished, there was a long silence. Then he looked towards her and caught her eye. He looked away again at once. She stood up and went towards the window. The starlings had disappeared.

"It's not true," she said simply. "I know it's not true—do you?" She turned to face him. "Do you know that the story you have just told me is not true," she repeated. "Perhaps you don't—didn't know Alex. If you did, you would have known it wasn't true. If you did know him, Mr Armstrong—" she paused wearily in a gesture of dismissal—"you are either stupid . . . or malevolent."

Essen, Tuesday Evening

Scholz was worried. In a darkened corner of the scruffy *Bierstube* he sat scowling with a thin glass of *Pils* clutched in his huge hands. He had just had a row with his wife over some trivial matter, and had stormed out into the evening gloom to drink and to think. He avoided the *Stammtisch* by the door where he usually met his friends for a game of cards. Seeing his mood, they had shrugged their shoulders and had gone on with their game.

All he had wanted to do was to be helpful. He had gone round to the Police Office, and told them what he had known. He had described to a detective the man he had given a lift, and at first they had appeared grateful. He had been kept waiting for a couple of hours, but they had kindly brought him a couple of *Würste* and some coffee when he had explained that he hadn't eaten since morning.

Then two men, somehow different, less military than the other policemen, had arrived, and had questioned him for a very long time. They had particularly pressed him on his description of his passenger. Scholz had said that he had been small, with neat, almost feminine hands. Was Scholz sure? The man the newspapers said that the police were looking for was tall and thin—an Italian labourer—who wouldn't have dainty hands surely? The peculiarly blurred photograph of the suspect they showed him couldn't remotely belong to Scholz's man, could it? Or could it? Had Scholz been drinking perhaps? Was he sure which parking lot was being talked about? Could he remember the man with any precision—it had been snowing heavily, hadn't it? Scholz had been tired. Was he sure? Was he sure?

Günter Scholz prided himself on being an honest man and a supporter of authority. Yes, he said, he was sure. He hadn't been drinking. Yes, the man had come from the van. He was certain that it was the same parking place. There might have been another van certainly, but then it must have been well hidden. The area wasn't very large. Then there had been all the blood on the seat in his cab. He had almost forgotten that. Sorry!

At that, one of the men had disappeared. The other said he was afraid Scholz would have to stay the night. Yes he could phone his wife and tell her not to worry.

They had wakened him at six in the morning. The blood on the seat apparently was of the same group as that of one of the bodies. Not conclusive, but . . .

The detectives' tone had changed overnight. They had almost seemed suspicious of him. Surely they didn't suspect . . . Otherwise he wouldn't have come forward? No, of course they didn't suspect Scholz. They would let him go soon, they promised. Yes, they were still looking for an Italian labourer. No, they weren't looking for the little man described by Scholz. "Why?", he had asked. None of his business. Not right to suppress his evidence, he suggested. They had been very angry at this. If he was to start spreading rumours of another man, a little man, it would be too bad, Herr Scholz. He wouldn't want trouble, would he? If he were to be difficult, then there might be some talk of what he did in the war. Yes, they did know a lot about him, didn't they? Only an ordinary, very young soldier then? Really? Where was it—just prison camp duties eh? Just took orders, really. Didn't like what he had to do? No, of course not, but hadn't he heard of war-crime trials? They were still going on, Herr Scholz. Wouldn't like that sort of thing to be dug up? Certainly not.

Scholz ordered another *Pils* and a glass of *Steinhäger*. Why the hell had he gone forward in the first place? He wouldn't do anything like that in a hurry again.

"Let me get this one for you. Herr Scholz, isn't it?" A fat heavy man was beaming down at him.

"I can put it on expenses you see," the stranger explained unasked.

"Who the bloody hell are you, and how do you know my name?" Scholz looked up through a haze of alcohol.

"Walt Tesco, pleased to meet you, Herr Scholz." A chubby hand was extended and ignored.

"If you're a bloody cop you can get stuffed. I've said all I'm going to say, and I won't give your game away whatever it is. It's not worth my while."

"Aha, so I was right." Tesco beamed with pleasure. "No, Herr Scholz, I'm not a policeman. Just a humble journalist with an eye open for a good story. I heard you might be here."

He sat down unasked beside Scholz, and when the

waiter appeared, he ordered another beer and *Schnapps* and paid for them both.

"What d'you want?" Scholz was still surly, but he accepted the drink.

"I have a little proposition to make to you," was the whispered reply. "All very confidential of course, Herr Scholz."

FOUR

Whitehall, Tuesday Evening

The benign portrait of some unknown former dignitary gazed down from its gilded frame. Apart from a large map-board, it was the only decoration in the room. The green-baize cloth of the conference table was littered with coffee cups, ashtrays and red-jacketed files. Twelve men and one woman were seated round the table. The heavy curtains were tightly drawn, shutting out the last light of the London winter afternoon. The neon light glowed through the cigarette smoke.

The mood of the meeting was tense, every face emphasizing the seriousness of the situation. "But we're not getting anywhere fast," thought Armstrong impatiently. He recalled what had been said about committees, that they reached a decision at the speed of the slowest member. Brander should have been pensioned off long ago. He was holding everything up, was more worried about what the Minister might do than getting on with deciding what should be done in the present situation. He had the irritating ability to produce red-herrings and get others to follow him after them.

Eventually the Director took charge. "Thank you, Brander, but I think we cannot spend any more time on how we handle the Minister. We can leave that to his Cabinet colleagues. We have, however, to carry out his instructions as given to Armstrong, to the best of our ability. At the same time, however, we still hold it to be essential to our interests to discover as much as we can about the other side's industrial capabilities. Obviously, Sonntag is not going to be the means of achieving this from now on, and we shall have to consider more, er, orthodox ways. But I think we must try, without perhaps broadcasting the fact, to discover where we slipped up, who killed our people, and how much the other side have discovered about Operation Sonntag as a whole. This is essential to the future of this organization.

"We are agreed," the Director continued, "that there must have been a leak, and indeed the evidence clearly indicates that someone very close to the operation, to put it bluntly, betrayed our people. We aren't permitted to advance any further with this project, and I must say here that I fully support the Minister in his decision, so let there be no more talk of how we can get round his order. But I do feel that we must, for the safety of this organization, try to find out who was responsible. May I, therefore, take it as approved, as I suggested earlier, that Armstrong here takes charge of this enquiry. I hope you will give him your fullest support."

There was a general murmur of agreement. Brander alone complained briefly that it was his section that dealt with security matters, but he was generally ignored in the livelier discussion which followed. Brander wasn't the most popular of colleagues; it was getting late and people wanted to go home.

Armstrong sensed the mood and spoke briefly. "I have arranged to fly to Germany tomorrow, Director.

It couldn't be left to our people on the spot, and besides it might even be with them—any leak, that is.

"One slight worry, Sir, which Miss Dixon may be able to help with." Armstrong looked at the middle-aged woman sitting at the far end of the table. Miss Dixon, a relic of war-time operations, had a mind that was far from a relic. That her own comparatively well-known sexual predelictions were tolerated by her employers was a reward for her indefatigable talent for finding out the more unsavoury details of people's lives and backgrounds. Almost every one of the twelve men seated round the table disliked her, but it was with a dislike controlled by a certain fear of her abilities.

"It's Alex's fiancée," he went on. "I broke the news to her this morning. She's obviously intelligent, and perhaps not unnaturally is reluctant to believe what the German press is saying. She doesn't credit her fiancé with having an affair with someone else's wife. She may try to find out something, and it may be worth keeping an eye on her and . . . drawing her off if she gets too near the truth."

Armstrong was aware as he spoke of a slight reaction inside himself at the thought of Miss Dixon setting to work on Miss Weinberg.

"You will let me have her details before you leave, Mr Armstrong?" Miss Dixon agreed.

Just a name on a piece of paper after all. . . .

Earls Court, Wednesday Evening

It was the worst sort of cheap hotel, somewhere off the Earls Court Road. The bedroom was scruffy, the furniture indifferent, and, if any heating was required by a guest, it was a matter of finding shillings to put in a meter before the electric fire would go on.

Walt Tesco hadn't any shillings, so he kept his overcoat on instead. It was only a base for the night after all, and it was his own fault if he had decided to economize. He shuddered involuntarily. He had become too used to the French and Italian Rivieras, chasing after film star gossip for the glossy German news magazine he worked for. This double-murder case was admittedly much more interesting, but it was hard work, and the going was slow.

Certainly there had been lots of clues, lots of loose ends at the start of the case, but now, in a funny way, they had started vanishing, as if someone, somewhere, was doing a cover-up job. Must be from pretty high up, judging by the things they had managed to suppress. That, come to think of it, was why he had decided to follow the story. His Chief Editor had given him the go-ahead, but since then he had played it very close to his chest. He didn't want any of his colleagues cashing in on what might be a major scoop. He had a nose for scandals, that's why they paid him so well.

Remarkable piece of luck stumbling on that driver, with his story of the little man who had been his passenger. Tesco had already come to the conclusion that the photograph the police had issued of a so-called "Italian labourer" had looked a bit contrived. Pure chance that he had been in the police station trying to get material on the story at the very moment Scholz was dismissed. But why were they doing this, why were they covering up, and for whom?

A little bit of spade work and a flying visit to the local Helmstedt police had uncovered another peculiar snippet. One young officer had gossiped a bit too freely to him about the fact that the man who had been killed was believed to be British. He had no passport, but he had carried a letter addressed to a girl friend or rather a fiancée in London. Odd that someone who was engaged should be busy sleeping with another woman, to the extent of getting himself brutally murdered by a jealous husband. Fiancés, Tesco felt, probably were the most loyal of men. They usually waited until they got married before they were unfaithful.

The young officer had even given him the name of the girl and told him that she lived in London. Tesco had flattered him. A journalist from a famous magazine paying him so much attention. Yes, he would see what he could do about getting the full address of the girl.

Tesco had telephoned the young policeman later. The reply had been terse. Obviously he had been warned off. But a name and a town had been enough in the past for a clever painstaking journalist. There couldn't be all that many girls of that name in London—especially with fiancés who had been murdered in Germany.

Tesco sat on the edge of the hard bed, thumbing his way through the heavy volumes of the London Telephone Directory which he had borrowed from the reception desk. He peered myopically at the tiny print and the unfamiliar names. Producing a little note-book, he wrote down a list of numbers and then went in search of a telephone box. The one in the hotel was out of order, the holes stuck with what seemed to be chewing-gum.

In Germany it would have been replaced straight away. But in Germany perhaps it wouldn't have happened.

He found a box at the corner of a street, glass broken, and evil-smelling inside. He pulled out a handful of sixpences and started telephoning.

Tesco was a patient man, a patience that comes of not moving fast, not wishing for too much exertion. But it was a struggle inside that box made for smaller men. He rang several numbers without success.

Eventually he got a man's voice which told him that pretty Miss Weinberg had recently left the flat and had gone to stay with her sister somewhere in North London. She was trying to save money, since she was about to get married. Was the caller a friend and didn't know she was engaged? The voice at the other end sounded suspicious. Been abroad, oh, that was it. Well in that case the address was somewhere about. Just one moment . . .

FIVE

Islington, Thursday Morning

The taxi deposited him at the corner of the street. He would walk the rest. Tesco always liked to get a picture of their environment before he met and talked to people.

It was raining slightly, and the street was deserted except for a few children playing with an old car tyre. They looked pretty dirty and wet; their mothers wouldn't be pleased.

Number 37 was a tall Victorian stuccoed house, four or five floors high, which had seen better days. He went up the few steps to the door, and looked down the little plastic name-list of occupants which was fitted beside the row of door bells. He pressed the button marked Donovan. As he waited for an answer, he turned slightly and looked up and down the street. A middle-aged woman, with almost masculine close-cropped grey hair, was walking along the pavement, obviously looking for a particular house. She carried a large black man's umbrella. She made to come up to Number 37 too, but then she saw Tesco standing at the door, seemed to hesitate slightly, then turned and purposefully walked on down the street.

He heard the electric catch on the door buzz and he pushed his way into the gloomy tiled hall. The door on the fourth floor was open, and at it stood a small child, whether boy or girl, he wasn't sure.

"What do you want?" it asked.

"Is your mother at home?"

"Mummy," it yelled through the door. "There's a big man with a funny voice to see you."

The mother appeared. "I'm so sorry to have kept you."

"Mrs Donovan?"

"Yes?"

"I wonder if I could speak to your sister, Miss Weinberg—just for a moment you understand. It's important." He fumbled in his wallet for his visiting card.

"Oh yes, I'll get her. But please don't, er, stay too long. She's just had a tremendous shock, you know, and isn't feeling up to visitors very much just now."

"Yes, I heard. That's why I came." She looked surprised at his remark.

"Who is it?" a girl's voice asked from inside the flat.

"Someone to see you, Jo. A Mr . . ."

"Tesco—Walt Tesco," he explained.

In the living-room he met the girl. He sized her up. She was pretty. He could already see the photographs of her in his magazine. The editor could think up some nice moving title for the story.

Mrs Donovan excused herself and shepherded the several children that had appeared on his arrival out of the room. Jo Weinberg shut the door.

"Can I help you?" Her face showed something of the strain she had been living through.

"Name is Walt Tesco, you may have read some of my stuff? No . . . ah, well. I'm a journalist you see. Excuse my English. I'm afraid it's a bit rusty."

"We can speak in German if you like—you are German, Herr Tesco, I presume?"

c

"Quite right. Quite right. You'll know my magazine, of course, if you don't know me." He handed her his card. "I'll speak in my bad English if you don't mind. It helps me set the scene," he started to joke, but her look silenced him.

"What can I do for you?" she asked coldly.

"It's your fiancé. I'm very sorry. I've been working on . . ."

"I am afraid that I have nothing to say to the press, especially the German press. As far as I am concerned, all they have been writing about Alex so far is a pack of lies. Let me show you out." Her outburst surprised them both. She walked towards the door.

Tesco made no move to go. "But I entirely agree with you, Miss Weinberg. Entirely. That's why I came. It's all been a pack of lies . . . so far, as you said."

She stopped and looked at him in amazement. "What do you mean? What's all this about?"

"You tell me. You tell me, Miss Weinberg. May I sit down?"

She gestured towards a chair. He lowered his large body slowly into it. She perched on a couch beside the window and stared at him impatiently.

"What do you mean, all lies?" she asked.

"What do *you* mean, Miss Weinberg?" he echoed.

"Don't play games with me Mr—Herr Tesco."

"I'm not playing. I'm trying to earn a living, and I'm trying to find out the truth. Like you, Miss Weinberg, I suspect that your fiancé didn't die as the result of what the French call a *crime passionelle*."

"I don't suspect it, I know it."

"Very well. We are agreed. I know it, too. I'm here to ask your help. I may be able to help you too. So let's get down to business." His manner was brusque.

"But you'll want to publish—I know your magazine. It will all sound so sordid—whatever the truth is."

"That's a harsh verdict, Miss Weinberg. It's not always the case. We do have our serious side too. We've exposed quite a few mistakes, deliberate and otherwise, in the judicial machine in recent years."

"But . . ." she began.

"The thing is, Miss Weinberg, do you want to know the truth or do you not? Do you want to live with a memory of a squalid slur on your fiancé's name? Do you? Of course you don't. We . . . er . . . need each other, so to speak. I tell you what. I'll clear my copy with you before I submit anything to the editor. That's a promise."

"How do I know if I can trust you?"

"You don't know. But you might as well take the chance. I'll go further and do the first exchanging of information, just to show I'm serious. I'll tell you, for example, what a man called Günter Scholz told me the other day. Do you mind if I speak in German now, it will help me remember the details?"

He had finished his part of the bargain by the time Mrs Donovan brought in some tea.

"You all right, Jo?" she asked anxiously.

"Yes." Jo was gazing thoughtfully out of the window. "Mr Tesco is being very helpful. Do you mind leaving us alone?"

Then she started talking of her life since she met Alex.

Occasionally, Tesco would make a note in his little black book.

She told of how they met at a party. Of how they had got to know each other so quickly. The story came pouring out. She realized what a relief it all was to tell everything even to this large flabby stranger. They had been in love. It hadn't been for long, but they had decided to get married nonetheless. They got on well together. They had been lovers, then they were friends. It seemed a good basis for a marriage, didn't it?

Alex worked with some Industrial Advisory Group, and spent a lot of his time abroad, mainly in Western Europe, but he often visited Communist countries as well. He never spoke about his work much, though. Come to think of it, she had done most of the talking. He listened most of the time, thoughtfully, drawing at the pipe he always smoked. Sometimes he had been a bit mysterious about his movements. She had teased him about it, and suggested he had a lover hidden away somewhere. Once he had caught hold of her tightly and said that she must never talk like that. He would never let her down. She had been a little frightened. Then he explained that sometimes his work was for the Government and therefore a little delicate. He had to keep his movements unknown from time to time. She asked with a laugh if he was spying while on his trips. He hadn't replied to that. But she thought she had guessed.

"That was it, Herr Tesco. Female intuition, that's all. I'm afraid I haven't been able to help very materially in your researches."

"But you have, Miss Weinberg—you have indeed. We

must keep in touch. Indeed we must. Where was it you said he worked? What was the address?"

"I'm afraid I only have the phone number."

"That will do, of course. Let me leave you my number as well. I go back to Düsseldorf tonight, but you can dial direct these days. I'm at your disposal any time— any time at all."

As he left the house he saw the military-looking lady with the short grey hair whom he had seen earlier. She was coming along the pavement towards the house. He walked away from her rapidly and turned the corner. On an impulse, he waited a moment and then looked cautiously round the corner into the street again. The woman was just going into the door of Number 37.

Chelsea, Friday Morning

It was some time before she accepted that someone was following her. Walking south along Sloane Street, the pavements were relatively uncrowded, and it became increasingly obvious. At first she thought it was someone attempting a pick-up. Surprisingly early in the day for that, but it had happened before.

She turned into Peter Jones at the corner of Sloane Square and took the lift to the furniture department. She and Alex had opened an account there. She wandered about among the easy chairs for some minutes and had almost dismissed her suspicion as stupid, when she caught sight of the man's reflection in a wardrobe mirror. A nondescript type in a brown felt hat and a grey mackintosh, he was studiously examining a large brass bedstead. Someone very persistent, or pure chance?

She put it to the test by going quickly down a floor to ladies' underwear. Then she waited, and, in a moment or two, saw him appear breathlessly at the foot of some stairs and look round uncertainly. He caught sight of her and turned away. There was no doubt about it now. She felt him watching her as she bought some unwanted stockings; and then, waiting for the assistant to bring her change, she turned hostilely towards him again. But by this time he was nonchalantly examining a pile of silk scarves.

She was annoyed now, but something inside her suggested caution. Pretending not to have noticed his interest, she took her change and walked quickly in his direction. Equally quickly he dropped the scarf he was holding and moved away from her. She stopped, and he hesitated, framed in a doorway. If it *was* an attempted pick-up, it was a very nervous one. Coolly she decided that she would play the game and continue to pretend that she hadn't noticed.

She took the lift to the ground floor and left the store. The King's Road was busy but she managed to make her way fairly quickly through the crowd. After a few hundred yards she stopped abruptly, pretending to look in a boutique window, and watched his reflection as he overshot her. He didn't stop or look in her direction, but a few shops further on he paused to window-gaze as well.

So it was a quite determined attempt to follow her. They, whoever they were, couldn't think much of her, having set such a clumsy operator on her tail. Perhaps she should try to catch up with him, question him . . . But again she was stopped by caution and a feeling that she might still be deluding herself.

She decided to take evasive action. Out of the corner of her eye she saw a Number Eleven bus halt for a pedestrian crossing nearby. She turned, darted across to it and jumped on board. Fortunately, the road was surprisingly clear ahead and the bus managed to lurch forward more or less immediately. Out of the back window she saw her tail frantically summon a taxi. Looking forward, she realized that the bus was going to get snarled up in traffic again pretty soon. She muttered to the conductress about having got on the wrong bus and as soon as it slowed down she jumped off again into the crowd.

A few hundred yards gained on her pursuer, perhaps more if he hadn't seen her disembark. She moved into a shop doorway and turned just in time to see the taxi shoot past. Its passenger was leaning forward on the edge of the back seat, talking urgently to the driver and pointing at the bus in front. He didn't even glance in her direction.

She went out on to the pavement again and stood watching until the taxi was out of sight. She felt oddly pleased with herself. Shoppers jostled irritably past her on the narrow pavement, but she didn't notice until an old workman pushing a hand-cart shouted at her not to block the way. She pulled herself together with an effort and turned into a nearby coffee shop. A little time was needed to think things out. She sat down at a table near the back and tried to relax.

For the moment she had felt childishly elated but the mood had quickly faded. Something about the man's behaviour, his movements in the taxi, told her that it was far from being a game. Here in London for some reason, she was being followed. He hadn't been very clever, but he wouldn't have expected her to notice him in the first place, nor thought that she might do something about it.

Alex, Armstrong, Tesco—and then Miss Dixon. It occurred to her that this incident was probably connected with the visit from the peculiar Miss Dixon. Right from the start she had been surprised at Miss Dixon's being a welfare officer. If she had worked in Alex's office, Miss Dixon would have been the last person she would have gone to with her troubles. Odd, too, of his office to have bothered themselves with her problems. After all, they hadn't been married. Still, at first she thought that it was meant kindly. Later, she wasn't at all sure that Miss Dixon, with her odd looks and embarrassing smile, hadn't been warning her off.

She had been questioned rather heartlessly by Miss Dixon. If by that time her feelings had not been numbed, she would have been hurt. Miss Dixon indeed seemed to say things in order to hurt. One could imagine her in boots with a stock-whip. Yet all the time she had said she was trying to help. Jo had given her the benefit of the doubt and hadn't asked her to leave. She had been asked to answer some surprisingly intimate questions about her relations with Alex, and naturally she had refused to reply. Miss Dixon had merely shrugged her shoulders, appearing content with the grudging statement that Alex had never talked about his work.

Then Miss Dixon had asked if she believed the story about how he died. Just like that, with no warning. But of course that man Armstrong must have told her. She hadn't looked at Miss Dixon as she replied, but she had felt her watching her like a hawk. She had almost begun automatically to repeat what she thought, but something made her stop. "Yes," she had said, "of course I didn't believe it at first, but now . . ." She had looked down at the carpet, regretting her inability to lie effectively, regretting even more that Miss Dixon wasn't being deceived.

Eventually Miss Dixon had left. It was an enormous relief when she was gone. How pleasant it had been to open all the windows and let in fresh air. Even as she had left, she had appeared ugly and almost threatening. What was it she had said? "Don't do anything precipitate, will you? If I can be of any help, do let me know." Then she had smiled. Miss Dixon's smile was the worst thing about her.

The parting warning made sense now. Presumably she was under some sort of surveillance. They knew where she lived, and when the man in the taxi reported that he had lost her, they would simply go back and wait for her to turn up at the house. If she wanted to do anything without them knowing, now was the only chance. She shivered slightly, and then abandoned her luke-warm coffee and went out into the King's Road once again.

SIX

Düsseldorf, Monday Afternoon

The airport loudspeaker system blared out incomprehensibly, alternately in English and German. The closed-circuit television cameras announced delays in all flights due to heavy snow on the runways. People and baggage scattered about the arrival hall gave its clinical lines a small amount of human warmth.

Jo Weinberg presented her passport rather nervously at the control desk. She was in Germany again for the first time for twenty-nine years. Not that she remembered leaving it. She had been only a few months old when friends had driven her, wrapped in blankets inside an old chicken-box, across the frontier to Switzerland, to join her refugee parents. They had been among the last to have got out.

She had always said she would never go back. It was irrational perhaps. It wasn't as if her half-Jewishness had intruded into her life very much; and she realized that the new Germany was very different from the old. Still, the stories of her parents, and the ones she had read about herself, had kindled some deep remembrance inside her.

The passport officer barely gave her passport a glance. She went into the baggage hall to collect her case. Now what? She had hardly thought beyond getting herself to Germany. She supposed the first thing to do would be to find a hotel and then contact Walt Tesco. But then? It was all so confusing.

She went to the airport restaurant and ordered a coffee. Not that she wanted one. They had had too many refreshments on the plane, while they were circling, waiting for clearance to land. But she wanted somewhere to think. She looked at her watch. Only an hour late, and for once at the end of a journey, there was no one waiting, no one expecting her—at least she hoped not. She thought back to Miss Dixon's visit and of her discovery that she was being followed. This had tipped the balance and was why she was back in Germany after such a long time. That it was important enough to arrange to have her followed suggested there was something to hide.

After dropping her tail in the King's Road, she had decided on an impulse to buy the air ticket to Düsseldorf as a precaution. That they had been waiting for her back at her sister's house had settled matters. She had been incensed, but had controlled herself and had tamely allowed them to follow her during the weekend. It must have been pretty boring for them which would explain in part the ease with which she got away without their noticing, in the early hours of the morning.

She forced herself back to the present. It was only four days yet it seemed ages since she had spoken with Tesco. Four days of feeling very much alone. She sipped her coffee nervously, paid, and went out and found a taxi to take her to an inexpensive hotel near the town centre.

Struggling with the unfamiliar German coins in the

telephone booth, she eventually got through to his office. Her German came surprisingly fluently.

"*Herr Walt Tesco, bitte.*"

"*Moment mal,*" came the operator's reply.

"Tesco here . . ."

"Hello. It's me, Jo Weinberg. I took you at your word."

"Where are you?" Tesco sounded cautious.

"Here in town. I've just flown in."

"Oh, er, yes." There was a long pause.

"Where and when can we meet?" Jo asked anxiously.

"Well, I'm, er, afraid that it's not as easy as that. I'm on . . . another job at the moment. Difficult to leave. You know how it is." Tesco sounded worried.

"But I've come all this way to see you, as we arranged last week. I appreciate that you're busy, but at least we can make an appointment for tomorrow."

"Yes. Yes, of course. It's just that—" suddenly the tone of his voice changed, and he whispered, "I've been called off your story. Too hot. But listen, I can't let you down. Meet me in three-quarters of an hour at the Europa Bar, corner of Goethe and Hauptstrasse. I'll try . . . *Nein,* I must have the photographs by tonight," Tesco abruptly shouted into the phone, and then slammed the receiver down. Jo realized that someone must have disturbed him. But it was all very odd. Tesco, fat and uncouth as he was, hadn't appeared to her as someone who would have been frightened off a story. She suddenly felt very much on her own, and in a panic she nearly decided to go no further, leave the whole thing covered up—whatever it was. That holiday she had told people about—she could really take it. . . . Then she re-established her self-control.

The Europa Bar was one of those cheap modern plastic and chrome affairs that were gradually overtaking the old-fashioned *Gemütlichkeit* of the traditional German *Bierstube*. She took a table in a corner, partly hidden from the door by a rack of coats. She ordered a *Pils*. She kept her coat on and the collar turned up. It was a sort of protection for her.

After a long quarter of an hour, Tesco came in. They shook hands quietly. He kept his coat on too, and without asking her, ordered two beers and two glasses of *Schnapps*.

"Sorry to keep you," he smiled apologetically. "It's a bit tricky now, and I had to give them the slip."

"What," she said incredulously. "Do you mean that someone is following you too?"

"Fortunately not very expertly. They presumably thought I was easy. But I've had a lot of experience dropping tails in my job. Nonetheless," he said looking nervously over his shoulder, "this is obviously serious, and I've got my job to think of, you know. I'm afraid that this is the only time we can meet, and I'll have to be quick. I'm sorry to let you down, but the day I got back, the Chief Editor got on to me and ordered me to drop it, drop the whole case. The order came via the magazine's owner, who is also very highly placed with the Government. 'In the interests of national security', was the spiel they gave me.

"I thought that despite the warning, I'd try keeping on with the case. One has other markets you know,

France, Italy and the like. But when I was following up something near Helmstedt, they dropped on me like a ton of bricks—the police that is—and kept me inside without charging me, for twenty-four hours, just to warn me, they said. If I tried to complain or talk to my lawyer, they said they'd pick me up again, put me inside and throw away the key. Thing is, I know that sort of lark can happen, even in a democracy. They let you out later, saying it was a case of mistaken identity—if you're lucky."

"My God. I can hardly believe it. But what's it all about? What's all so serious?"

"Surely," Tesco replied evenly, "you haven't forgotten that it's something so serious that your fiancé got bumped off. That's how serious it is. And I'll tell you two things for a start. First, he wasn't some married woman's lover, 'cause that woman wasn't married, and secondly, he met his death somewhere a long way away from Helmstedt, beyond that string of barbed wire and concrete they call the Iron Curtain, to be a little more precise. And I think that a lot of people high up on both sides of the Curtain know this, but are determined not to let it become common knowledge. Why? Don't ask me. Now I'll tell you something else interesting . . ."

"Not now you won't." The two green leather-coated policemen had walked up to the table without either Tesco or the girl noticing. "I have instructions, Herr Walter Tesco, to arrest you for suspected theft. I must ask you to come with us without disturbance."

Tesco seemed to crumple up inside his coat. He shot an appealing glance at Jo, who stood up angrily and said, "Leave him alone. What's he done. Why are . . ."

"This is none of your affair. Please keep out of it, and let us get on with our job." The elder of the two policemen smiled at her almost kindly.

"But what right . . ."

"Very well, then," said the policeman noting her accent, "where are your papers, your passport?"

"At my hotel."

"Then you come along too."

"But I'm a British subject. I demand to see the British Consul."

"We'll see about that later."

A man, presumably a detective, swathed in a brown gaberdine coat, appeared at the door of the cell, along with a man whose haircut and moustache could not have allowed him to be anything but British.

"Miss Weinberg," the Consul said, "I am afraid that we are in agreement with the Federal German police. Your papers and passport are not in order. You must leave the country by the first available flight tomorrow. Until this time you may stay here in the police station or, if you like, return with me to the Consulate."

"But my papers are in perfect order. I just had them checked," Jo said defiantly.

"I'm sorry." The Consul did indeed look sorry. "I am not prepared to argue. Would you like to come, or stay here? You might be more comfortable with us." He looked round the cell disapprovingly.

"I'll come," she said helplessly, after a few seconds pause.

SEVEN

Helmstedt, Monday Afternoon

Even after the army driver slipped the Land-Rover into four-wheel drive, the wheels spun helplessly on the powdery snow. When a few fruitless minutes of work with a spade failed to get the vehicle moving, Armstrong and the young army officer left on foot to cover the last remaining kilometre to the zonal border.

The going was slow. The snow had drifted across the track between the pine trees, and it took them nearly half an hour to reach their objective.

"There it is, just to the left of that guard tower. It's frozen hard at the moment of course."

Armstrong could make out the dip in the snow where the little canal ran. He followed it with his eye till it hit the fence and the barbed wire of the Curtain. Beyond was the inevitable stretch of open ground, which, unless covered by snow, would be kept perpetually ploughed and raked.

"Keep back in the trees, Sir. It doesn't matter much as they'll think we're just doing a routine check, but there is no particular need to draw attention to ourselves." He scanned the guard tower with his binoculars. "Aha! Too late. They've spotted us, but never mind. Would you like to have a look?"

Armstrong took the binoculars and looked towards the tower. He could clearly see the two *Vopos* staring back at him. Imperceptibly, he moved his focus towards the canal. Beside it he could make out the gate in the wire. To the casual observer, if any came that way, it would be to let workmen or guards through to repair the fence. But they now knew that it had other uses as well.

"We discovered it just by chance. Routine exercise. We were watching the tower for hours without being seen. Then we saw them coming. Two big chaps and a little fellow. They were carrying a large box. The little chap stayed this side to keep watch, and the others went back and brought another similar box across. Then the van came. There wasn't much snow about. It had just started, in fact."

"Why didn't you arrest them?"

"I'm afraid we'd no orders to do so. We weren't on patrol. It was me in charge, you see," he added apologetically. "We hadn't any warrants. But we did try to follow them. Then we lost contact, and I went back to make my report. If I'd taken the law into my own hands and picked them up, there would have been hell to pay. It might have been something we had arranged, or the Federal Government. We have strict instructions. People round here are very nervous about stirring up border trouble."

"Quite right. You did quite right. I'll tell them so. You got the number of the van, of course?"

"Of course, Sir. Thank you very much indeed. I appreciated something very odd was going on, but . . . Are you finished, Sir?"

"Yes, it's bitterly cold. Let's go."

The two men turned and went back up the track

between the trees. The going was difficult, and neither of them spoke for some minutes. The powdery snow blew down on them from the pine trees as they went. Then suddenly, Armstrong, who had been walking a little behind the other man, stopped in his track.

"Hold it! Not so fast, Lieutenant, there's something peculiar going on."

"What d'you mean, Sir?" The other man paused and looked back at him enquiringly.

"There on the left—see the tracks—these footprints. They're new. They weren't there when we came were they?"

"No, Sir. But it's probably some woodman." The Lieutenant shrugged indifferently and made to continue.

"Not coming from the wire, Lieutenant. They stopped behind that clump over there, then they go over to these trees. See? There are several sets of prints. Someone was and probably still is watching us."

"I agree it's spooky right up against the Curtain, Sir, but I've been here hundreds of times. There's probably some innocent explanation. You're right of course. It's odd, and I'll send in a report when we get back. People seem to have come over—perhaps refugees—they still manage from time to time." The Lieutenant was used to over-excited visitors. This was his territory.

"Right next to a guard post, Lieutenant? Try again. And you've just been telling me what you saw the other day. That's why we came here in the first place, remember?"

"I should have . . ." The Lieutenant, now a little abashed, looked around furtively.

"Never mind. Let's get back to the Land-Rover.

Whoever they were, they've probably gone by now." Armstrong didn't feel like listening to apologies.

They walked on again in silence, both men occasionally glancing about them. The track led back through the plantation of pine trees. The other footprints stretched ahead of them, still very fresh despite the blown snow.

Armstrong wondered vaguely whether they had any particular significance. He had a feeling that whoever else was there it might be something to do with him. It was too much of a coincidence. He had reported back to London that he was going to do the recce, so quite a few people would know he was there.

"There seems to be a welcoming party three or four hundred yards ahead," the Lieutenant's excited voice broke into his thoughts. "Looks as if we'll solve your mystery, Sir."

They stopped, and the Lieutenant produced his binoculars. Some whitened figures were standing in the middle of the track ahead.

"Four of them, Sir. They're coming towards us, spreading out slightly. Looks a bit odd. They're in civvies. Not army or border guards."

"You've got a pistol?" Armstrong had taken the binoculars and was peering through the trees at the men.

"No, Sir. It's in the Land-Rover."

"Then let's get out of here damn quick."

"But we're on the Western side. There's nothing to worry about, Sir. We'd better get back, the driver will be . . ." The Lieutenant was a bit exasperated at Armstrong's nervous behaviour.

"That's an order. They've all got rifles. Look, you can

see now without the binoculars and they're not hunting
guns either. For some reason these men are after us.
Into the trees. We'll be less easy to find."

The Lieutenant had begun to think that Armstrong
had gone off his head and was about to try to pacify him,
when a shot rang out. They both automatically fell flat
in the snow.

"What the bloody?" the Lieutenant grunted.

"Right, now are you convinced? We go together."
They quickly picked themselves up and ran into the pines.
There were no further shots, but the four were less than
two hundred yards away now.

Bending low beneath the branches of the closely
planted trees, they moved away from the track as best
they could. Armstrong felt very much out of condition
and was soon gasping for breath.

"If we have time, Sir, I can have a chopper from
Helmstedt down at the wire in five minutes." The
Lieutenant had produced a pocket transmitter. "The
pilot will find us only if we're at the open strip by the
Curtain, so we'd have to bear that way."

"Very well. But quickly." Armstrong was glad of the
rest.

The Lieutenant spoke urgently into the mouthpiece.
The radio crackled softly, and Armstrong could hear
the helicopter ops room asking for directions.

"Finished? They're close behind." They could both
hear the sound of men's voices.

They ran on again. Armstrong still breathlessly,
struggling for air, the Lieutenant jogging along comfortably beside him. The trees were thinning out.

"It's risky here. They'll spot us easily without more cover."

"Not to worry, Sir." The officer seemed to be enjoying himself now. "Behind those young trees over there is the strip and the Guard Post. We can lay up there and the new pines are planted so close that they'll help hide our tracks. The chopper won't be long. It'll just follow the Curtain down. They're on twenty-four-hour call. Lucky I had this radio gadget with me. We've just had them issued. Bloody efficient and about time too—sorry, you O.K., Sir? Think you can make the distance?"

Armstrong would have said something rude, but decided to conserve his breath. His look was enough to stop further conversation.

They reached the trees and crashed their way through. Just short of the far edge, Armstrong thankfully threw himself down in the snow, trying soundlessly to fill his exhausted lungs. The Lieutenant dropped easily beside him.

"Good spot, Sir. Well chosen. Right at the Curtain and with any luck they'll think we've gone the other way. We're perfectly positioned to dart out and signal when the chopper appears."

Armstrong nodded briefly, and again there was silence. Then they heard the crashing and occasional voices of their pursuers. They seemed very close and the two men lay still. Above the noise of the voices they gradually became aware of another sound and then the helicopter appeared low over the trees.

The Lieutenant waited a moment before he jumped out into the open.

"No! Stop!" Armstrong shouted a vain warning which coincided with the sound of a shot. The Lieutenant seemed to pirouette gracefully before falling in a heap on the open snow.

The gunman and his colleagues now seemed to become aware of the helicopter. They had been too intent on their prey to notice it before, but they did now, and it was obviously outside their brief to engage in a major battle. As Armstrong cautiously emerged and went over towards the Lieutenant, he saw four figures running to the gate that had appeared in the Curtain—a gate just to the left of the dip where the little canal ran.

Düsseldorf, Tuesday Morning

"No, the Lieutenant had a clean wound in the knee. It seems to have been a definite attempt at kidnapping or assassination, presumably aimed at me, and they knew precisely where I was to be found. I almost gave them it on a plate."

Armstrong eased himself off Captain Hermes' desk and, declining one of the proffered cigarillos, went on: "Who told them—that's question one. Why they wanted me—that's question two. You'll have to leave me to work on both."

"But why, Mr Armstrong, didn't they take you by surprise when you first went to the wire? It would have been easy."

"Because it might, as later proved the case, be more dangerous there. We watch the whole length pretty closely. No, if they took us a little bit inland, then they could bring us across the Curtain when things were absolutely clear."

"And they were a bit behind the time with their information on the army's new emergency procedures."

"Precisely. The Lieutenant had only had the transistor for a week. . . . Now, we'd better get back to the routine enquiries."

Captain Hermes was obviously excited at the prospect of a major security case. More fun than the routine stuff. Armstrong thought he'd better start taking the heat off. Too many people were in on the act already. He didn't want it to become a purge. He started to play it cool, helped by his inadequate knowledge of German. This slowed things up.

"Where's the van?"

"In the garage outside, Mr Armstrong."

"Finger-prints?"

"Lots, though none we've been able to trace. They don't belong to the two people in the van. In any case we don't set much store by this line of approach, since the steering-wheel and door-handles have been wiped clean. Probably the other marks don't matter."

"Anything else?"

"No, except that there are new, heavy-duty tyres on the vehicle, presumably to get it over the rough ground by the border."

"Presumably."

"We've picked up the journalist again, Mr Armstrong. He was getting to be a nuisance."

"I'd like to see him—alone, if possible."

"I'll have to get authority for that."

"Then get it."

"Yes, Mr Armstrong."

"Oh, and I'd like to interview the lorry-driver."

"Scholz?"

"That's the man. Please arrange it as soon as possible. There's not much time."

"Immediately, Mr Armstrong." The police captain saluted and left, somewhat chastened by Armstrong's unforthcoming attitude. He had hoped for something more glamorous.

Armstrong sat down at the desk, mentally going over the ground. Earlier on, before the Helmstedt incident, he had thought that he couldn't get far with his enquiries this side of the Curtain. Now he wasn't sure. The agents working for Sonntag on the other side were lying low at present and would do so till they got further orders. For the time being he could forget about them. The attempt to pick him up had demonstrated that the leak was nearer at home, either locally or in London—probably the latter. He would be better to return and start again.

Nevertheless, while he was here he could build up some sort of picture of what had happened. He doubted very much if interviewing the driver and Tesco would bring out anything, but it was worth the try. He might get a lead on the "little man", though doubtless he would be someone pretty low-level. The two bigger men, the corpse-bearers, weren't worth following up. They had probably gone back into the Zone. But why had the little man stayed beside the van waiting for the chance of a stray lift? That was surely risking things, or was it just bad organization? And why had he gone on to Hanover? Why hadn't he gone back too, after delivering the goods? It was pointless to speculate without something more positive to go on.

Captain Hermes brought in a large flabby man. This must be the gossip journalist. It couldn't be the long-distance lorry driver.

"Thank you. Would you mind leaving us alone." The policeman left reluctantly, shutting the door rather too noisily behind him.

"How do you do. My name's Armstrong. Do you mind if I speak in English? A cigarette? They're English."

Tesco, with new-found courage, ignored the offer: "You can speak in whatever bloody language you like. I'm not saying anything. You can do your own work. I'm a free citizen, being held against my democratic rights. Just wait till my editor hears about this."

"I understand he already has. He's washed his hands of you."

"I don't believe it. My editor isn't afraid of the police."

"We're a bit more than that, you know, Herr Tesco. We've got everything lined up against you. You would be advised not to fight."

Tesco crumpled quickly. His courage hadn't lasted very long. "O.K., O.K., I'll be good. You must have high-up friends. What do you want to know? Not that I've got very far. You lot saw to that."

Tesco was right. He hadn't got very far. He'd discovered that the jealous husband story was a put-up affair. He'd found out who Alex was, and who his companion had been. He knew that they worked far away from each other, and guessed, correctly, that they had never met. He presumed that the other side had done the whole thing as some sort of warning that the West were getting too curious. He had been very clever.

"But I hear you went to London. What for?"

"That's where your Alex came from, didn't he? I was following up a line there. I saw his fiancée; nice girl."

"Miss Weinberg?"

"Right."

"And . . ."

"Nothing. She knew nothing. That's all."

"O.K., Tesco. Thanks a lot. If you promise to be good, I'll get you out straight away. But you've been warned."

"Thanks for nothing. But I'll be glad to get home."

"Oh, one final question, Tesco. Why did you carry on and give the police the slip? Why was it so important to you to go back to the case, once you had been warned? Why did you deliberately try to throw off the officer who was, er, protecting you? Wasn't one twenty-four hours inside enough?"

"One thing, I don't like being tailed. Nobody does. The other, I was sorry for the girl."

"What girl? Miss Weinberg?"

"Yes. Didn't they tell you? She phoned me up and asked for my help. I may be a mere gossip columnist, but I couldn't let her down. They picked us up together."

"What? Do you mean she—Miss Weinberg—was here in Germany?"

"Was? Still is, as far as I know. Game girl that. It

would have made a beautiful story. Leave her alone, though, won't you?"

Armstrong was already reaching angrily for the phone. "Get me Hermes . . . Hello, Hello . . . that Hermes? . . . Good. You've got a girl, a Miss Weinberg . . . Yes, that's the one, along with Tesco. Why the hell wasn't I told? . . . Damn Miss Dixon . . . Yes of course she's to do with it. . . . What? . . . The British Consul? . . . Why the hell? . . . Back to London? . . . When's the plane? Have I got time to get to the airport? . . . Good, we'll try. Get me a car straight away."

Armstrong slammed the receiver down and stood up. An idea was floating somewhere inside him. "Thanks a lot, Herr Tesco. . . . Oh, yes, I'll see you're all right."

"You'll be good to her, won't you. She's a nice kid. I shouldn't have said anything about her." Tesco looked genuinely worried.

"I'll tell you something, Herr Tesco." Armstrong paused briefly at the door. "Don't tell anyone, but I think that Miss Weinberg may eventually be just a little pleased to see me."

Düsseldorf, Tuesday Lunchtime

"British European Airways regret to announce that their flight BE549 to London has been delayed due to the late arrival of the incoming plane. A further announcement will be made at twelve-thirty hours. In the meantime, all passengers travelling on this flight are invited to go to the B.E.A. information desk with their boarding cards, where they can obtain luncheon vouchers for use in the airport restaurant." The female voice was cold and meticulous.

In the airport police office, it was warm and stuffy. Jo sat on a low leather chair. It hadn't been designed for sitting on, she decided. But it looked nice. Beside her sat a tall, pale young man, Vice-Consul MacHerbert to be precise. He was trying to talk to her. He was friendly enough. Only recently married, and his wife entertaining the lunch guests by herself, he explained. But he was enough of a married man to be intrigued by his task of seeing that beautiful Miss Weinberg got her plane—and no mistakes to be made or there would be trouble—that's what the Consul himself had said.

"Like a cigarette? They're duty free, don't worry."

"No, thank you. Very kind, but I don't feel like smoking." She smiled tiredly at him. It was all too much. It was all a romantic attempt that had misfired. But what could she do? What did someone in her position do? Write to her Member of Parliament, she supposed. Why the hell didn't that young man stop talking to her? Didn't he see she was tired?

She closed her eyes momentarily and didn't see the two men come into the room. They looked round uncertainly, and then one whispered to the other: "That's her . . . over there."

Mr Vice-Consul MacHerbert looked up and saw the two men. "Can I help?" he asked in German. He was very proud of his German.

"Mr MacHerbert?" One of the men addressed him in English. At the voices, Jo looked up too.

"Yes?" said the young man.

The man who had addressed him, showed him a little red card. There was a photograph inside it. He stood up when he had read the details on it. He looked excited.

Jo looked vaguely at the arrivals, and then gradually, through her tiredness, she focused on the one that she recognized from before.

"Good morning, Miss Weinberg. I'm glad we caught you," Armstrong said.

"You had caught me already."

"I didn't mean that." Armstrong was abruptly precise. "I meant before the plane left. Luckily it's delayed." She looked back at him without comprehension.

Armstrong turned to the young man. "I'm afraid there has been a mistake. Thank you very much. You may go now."

"But I have strict instructions . . . from the Consul . . ."

"They're changed. Take my word for it. Or, if you prefer, ask Captain Hermes here." Armstrong was brusque. "I repeat, there's been a mistake."

The policeman spoke to the young man quickly in German. Eventually they compromised, and the German and the Vice-Consul went to find a phone to seek the necessary authority. Armstrong and the girl were left alone.

Neither of them spoke for some moments. Then Armstrong said, "I'm sorry about this. You are quite free to stay if you wish."

"You seem to have a certain amount of say in the matter, Mr Armstrong."

"It's a matter of contacts. I just happened to hear . . ."

"Of course. Quite the knight errant."

Armstrong frowned. "I thought that some help might be required."

"Help for you, or help for me?"

"Perhaps both of us, if you like."

"You need my help?" She exaggerated her genuine surprise.

"That could be."

"But perhaps I don't want to help."

"That would be a pity . . . for both of us."

"You did say that I was free, didn't you?"

"Of course."

"And no conditions, like with poor Herr Tesco?"

"I'm afraid that there are degrees of freedom."

"Is that a threat?" she asked. Her tiredness was gone and she was on her mettle. The colour was rising in her cheeks.

Armstrong was sensitive enough to notice the danger signal. "Can I get you a cup of coffee?"

"Surely tea, Mr Armstrong. Isn't it tea that true-blue English drink in times of stress." She mocked him, but she was still angry. Before he had arrived she had given up. The people she had been dealing with were minor officials. It wasn't their fault, her predicament. But now she had one of the principals to get her teeth into. She wasn't going to slip away just like that, at least not with the threat of a dog leash round her neck which would or could be pulled, when she reached the limit of her particular degree of freedom.

"Thank you very much. I'll take up your offer of something to drink. But need we stay at the airport? I do hate airports, don't you, Mr Armstrong?" She smiled slightly, to take some of the anger away, but she would play hard to get, whatever it was they wanted.

"I have a car outside, waiting. What about your baggage?"

"Perhaps you could have it taken to the Stern Hotel. I think I'll stay on for a bit, now that I'm allowed to. Shall we go?"

They sat together in the back of the car. There was a glass screen between them and the police driver. Neither of them spoke as they drove along the stretch of autobahn to the town.

At the outskirts, Armstrong suddenly said, "I almost forgot, I've got someone I still have to see at the police station. Would you mind if we went there first. I don't like keeping people waiting."

"What's this? Is this your way of taking me in again? The mouse on a string act?"

"You mustn't be so suspicious, Miss Weinberg. I'm trying to do a job; I forgot about someone who's there, and I thought, I think, that you might just be interested in what he has to say, too. But just as you like."

"O.K., O.K., I'll tag along. But I want that drink you promised, sometime. And I don't want tea now." She settled back in the seat and closed her eyes. Armstrong left it at that.

The car pulled into the yard at the back of the police station. They got out and walked into the building. "I suggest you wait in the room next door while I talk to him. We can arrange it so that you can hear everything."

"Who are you going to be talking to?" Her curiosity

got the better of her for an instant, and simultaneously, Armstrong realized that she would almost certainly play along with the scheme that was gradually forming itself in his mind. The thing was to get her hooked. Then there wouldn't be too much difficulty, so long as she kept to his conditions.

"The man is a driver, a fellow called Scholz. Tesco probably told you about him. Well, I think we've got his whole story, but you might like to listen carefully to him nonetheless. It will bring you in at the beginning of the story, or the end, depending on how you look at it."

She listened. She had heard it all before. But somehow it focused her attention. She began to think, rather than just react. She also began to realize that she was no longer simply Alex's fiancée bent on some melodramatic spree. She was on the chase, or nearly. Armstrong would have been pleased at how quickly she had bitten.

EIGHT

Chelsea, Wednesday Evening

Walking along the dull stretch of the King's Road before it hits the World's End, Brander pulled the collar of his tweed coat up to protect himself a little from the seasonal drizzle. He limped slightly. An old war wound, he would explain if asked. It hardly tallied with his history of helping run the meat-rationing at the Ministry of Food during the war, and the truth had something to do with a double-decker bus.

He was angry and determined at the moment; and when it came to being vindictive, rather in line with his ability to lay red-herrings, Brander could lay claim to a surprising talent. He was going to be vindictive now. He was going to expose that young upstart Armstrong for what he was worth. One would think from all the messages that were pouring back from Germany that the man ran Security Department.

But Brander also knew that he was coming to the end of his time in the game. They had cottoned on to the fact that he had been rather irregularly enlisted—it had been connected with a black market operation in bread in the late forties, and with the Treasury purse strings being pulled ever tighter under this latest Government spending squeeze, he was intelligent enough to realize that his would be one of the first heads to roll. But that did not stop him looking for revenge, revenge on the presumptuous upstarts like Armstrong who were pushing him out.

But what could he do on his own? He knew the Director now treated him with less respect than was his due. His contributions during committee meetings were too often brushed aside, and his minutes were ignored. If this particular piece of revenge was to come off, he needed an ally; and who better than the invincible Miss Dixon?

It was because Miss Dixon had been for once less than invincible, that Brander was making this unaccustomed foray into the outer fringes of Chelsea. He had been working late (conscientious to the last, he told himself), and had read the evening's reports as they came in, rather than waiting till the morning. He had noted with growing anxiety, that there were indications of ever wider circles of leaks on the East European network. Two more agents were believed arrested in Dresden, and a third had disappeared, believed captured. He could imagine the Director's face in the morning. He would be summoned. The finger of blame would be ever so politely pointed. Another nail would be in the coffin of his retirement. He had to organize his defences, and quickly.

Then, almost hidden among the pile of reports, had been one from Armstrong in Germany. It had been sent in code through commercial channels. With the growth of international trading relations, the organization could most safely bury their messages in the vast mass of commercial cables. No monitoring service could cover everything. Embassy channels were too difficult and too slow. This particular cable contained a sentence about a girl. Brander vaguely remembered her being discussed at a meeting on the Sonntag affair. The sentence, drafted in annoyance by Armstrong, doubtless when he had been tired, criticized Miss Dixon in no uncertain terms, for letting the girl, Miss Weinberg, get away. The details didn't matter to Brander. The accusation did. Miss Dixon wouldn't be pleased if she knew. In the normal course of events she wouldn't know. Administration, who distributed the telegrams, always kept their eyes open for things that might cause bad feelings within the group. Bad for morale, the telegram would be steered away from where Miss Dixon could see it. Administration were the only people, apart from her superiors, who need know that she had slipped up.

Brander walked as fast as his limp would let him. His hand kept going up to his inside pocket to reassure himself that the photostat of the cable was still safe. He was panting slightly when he reached the house he was looking for. He turned in a black iron gate and down some steps to the basement.

A solitary light burned outside. The brass plate announced the "Club Sappho". It was useful being Head of Security, one knew where one's colleagues could be found. Brander rang the bell.

A young man opened the door. When he saw Brander he looked angry, and said: "Sorry, members only," in a high-pitched voice. Brander realized with a slight shock that the man was a woman. The door began to shut.

"But . . . I know that, but I must speak urgently with Miss Dixon. It is most important."

The door opened a fraction. "Who did you say?"

"Miss, er, Frances Dixon." He remembered her first name with an effort. He had never heard anyone dare call her by it, even in an organization where first names were commonplace. "My name's Brander."

"Oh, if you insist. I'll go and see." The door slammed in his face. After about two minutes, when Brander, now very wet since the drizzle had turned to rain, was just about to ring again, the door opened once more. "O.K. She says that you've to come in. But you can't stay. Members—women members—only, you know."

He was ushered into a darkly-lit hall hung with heavy velvet curtains, which reminded him of his Edwardian youth. The air was heavy with a peculiar mixture of scent and cigar smoke.

"You may leave your coat here. She's in the far room. But you can't stay, remember." The man-woman looked at him curiously, and then disappeared towards the sound of music and talking behind a curtained door.

He looked round disapprovingly. He remembered the confidential reports on Miss Dixon that he had once seen. Despite the information they contained, the Director had written in his spidery handwriting: "No action to be taken." That had been that.

Leaving his coat hanging alongside a row of military macintoshes and expensive furs, he walked cautiously towards the door at the end of the corridor and went in.

Miss Dixon was obviously slightly drunk. Dressed in a severe tweed suit, she was sitting upright on a red velvet chaise-longue, a whisky tumbler in her hand. Beside her sat a little blonde woman, who, the moment Brander entered, got up, scowled angrily at him and left hurriedly. Miss Dixon didn't seem to notice.

"Evening, Brander. What d'you want? Found my hideaway have you?" She spoke precisely, as if anxious not to slur her words.

Brander shuddered. His own private life was the dullest imaginable. People believed he must have some vices tucked away, somewhere. It wasn't true. All his vices were obvious.

"Miss Dixon . . ." he began. His throat was dry. He hadn't bargained on this. "I have to speak to you urgently."

"What's biting you, Brander?"

"I wonder . . . if we could talk a minute."

"That's what we're doing, aren't we? Sit down, man. Sit down. Damn it, where's Liz gone? You've driven her away, I expect." She looked around enquiringly and then shrugged indifferently. "Never mind, have a drink. Help yourself over there. There's plenty. We've got to spend the pittance the Government pays us somehow, haven't we. This is my way. What's yours, Brander? Men? Little girls? Oh, never mind. Have a drink."

Brander didn't argue, but helped himself self-consciously to a large whisky. He gulped it down.

"Now, relax, once you're here. It's against club rules, but what the hell. It's not often my male colleagues visit me." For the first and last time in his life, Brander heard Miss Dixon laugh. It was a memorable event.

"I must insist, Miss Dixon."

"Insist on what, Brander? Out with it. And quickly. I was in the middle of entertaining, and you'd better have something to make up 'for spoiling my evening."

Brander produced the photostat from his pocket and gave it to her. "You know what that means," he said. "Armstrong's getting a bit beyond himself."

"And you thought you'd get me to help you do something about it? Is that it?"

"I thought that we should perhaps, er, join forces to . . ."

"To bring him down. I see. Well I'll be blunt with you, Brander. I don't much like you or your type, and I don't suppose that you're falling over with love for me." She smiled. "But I don't like being blamed for things by young men like him. So I'm on. Now continue!" She had sobered up surprisingly quickly.

Brander took another gulp of whisky to camouflage his relief and then gathered himself together. "I gather Armstrong hasn't been keeping too close to his brief either. I mean," he said hurriedly as he saw Miss Dixon's look of annoyance, "he hasn't been doing what he was told to do. He is, I understand, recruiting the same Miss Weinberg to help find the, er, leak in the organization, and to clear up the whole affair generally. He's asked permission for the sub-operation, and it's been approved by the Director, since the girl is a new face, and if she's picked up, she can always argue that she's looking for the background to her fiancé's murder."

"The lone wolf, eh?" Miss Dixon was alert now. "But what can we do about it if the Director has given his blessing?"

"That's only at official level. Think what the Minister would say . . ."

"Are you proposing, Brander, that we drop everyone in it, by any chance? That's some suggestion. Quite a surprise coming from someone like you, from one of the pillars of the Establishment."

Brander ignored the insult. "Look at the telegram again, Miss Dixon. Not very nice for anyone is it? A little purge at the top would do no one any harm, would it? At least not you or me?"

"My God, you're a schemer, Brander! What's biting you? Oh, I know. They're going to retire you, is that it? Come to think of it, I did hear some gossip that that was the way the wind was blowing. This Sonntag thing must be about the last straw, mustn't it? This is your last chance."

Brander looked worried for an instant. Perhaps he had misjudged Miss Dixon's reaction. Now she would spill the dirt, and that would be him really out. He would lie, of course. He would never have said such a thing— and to Miss Dixon? It was preposterous! He was the pillar of the Establishment, just as she had said. But despite his protestations, even if they believed him, it would be another nail . . .

"Relax, Brander. I'll play. But not on your terms, nor for your sake, believe you me. There are other things, more important things than your petty spites I could tell you about. Perhaps the time has come." Miss Dixon stretched out on the couch, gazing up towards the vermilion ceiling. Brander, in his relief, poured himself another whisky, unasked.

"Leave it, Brander. We need clear heads. Now listen . . ."

NINE

Outside in the Ku'damm, the student demonstration was in full swing. The shouting, the police sirens, the continuous chanting—"Ho, Ho, Ho Chi Minh! Ho, Ho, Ho Chi Minh!"—could be heard clearly in the almost deserted café. With a squeal of brakes, an armoured vehicle, a water cannon mounted on top of it, drove quickly by.

The little man sat at the table by the window, a coffee pot and an empty cup beside him. He frowned disapprovingly at the noise. They didn't understand what it was all about. Some of them had the right ideas, but they lacked discipline and direction. That would have to come. In the meantime, he supposed, they were a useful distraction for the authorities, so long as they didn't become counterproductive in their anarchy.

The waiter hovered above him, and reluctantly he ordered another pot of coffee. He looked at his watch. It was only half an hour overdue. He had to give it a full hour before leaving.

He watched the waiter without thinking. The man was indescribably slow. Every few paces he would give a little shuffle as if about to break into a run. But the speed never came. When the coffee eventually arrived, it was tepid. It was sent back. The little man couldn't stand inefficiency; besides, it helped pass the time.

A new pot of coffee arrived. He poured himself a cup, unwrapped a cube of sugar, but instead of putting it in the coffee, he ate it. Then he sat back in his chair, and, producing a nail-file from his pocket, proceeded to manicure his already perfect nails. After each stroke, he would hold his hand away from him and inspect his work. An elderly lady sitting at a table opposite glared at him.

He noticed a small cut on the back of his forefinger. How had that happened? It was bleeding slightly and he dabbed at it with a handkerchief. The bloodstains spread across the white linen, and he shuddered. The sight of blood had always made him feel slightly sick. That was why the whole business with the two in the van had been so upsetting. They had left him to pick up the bits as usual. It had been messy and unnecessary.

He had warned them. So had the London source. That particular man and the woman had been the wrong ones to try the experiment on. London had said that the man at least was temperamentally unsuited, and that had proved correct. Much better to brainwash, indoctrinate, —whatever the in-word was—and try to infiltrate people who weren't as experienced as they had been. The psychiatrist had been fooled. They had played along just as he himself would have done in similar circumstances and then, predictably, they had tried to escape. All so clumsy and they had nearly succeeded. Only a stray mine at the Curtain had stopped them.

After that he had suggested they be quietly buried, that they disappear with minimal fuss. But Authority wanted them used to the full. The bodies had to be sent back as a warning—in his view a pointless gesture of what would certainly be presumed to be senseless brutality.

Still he had taken them, only to have the van Authority provided him with break down before he could get it to the Hanover Consulate to dump the bodies. At times the System was as inefficient as the Capitalist one was made out to be.

From Hanover he had reported back by cable. The message came to await further instructions in West Berlin. He was still waiting two weeks later. Was he in disgrace? He wasn't too worried at the thought. They could hardly blame him, and in the meantime, West Berlin had its compensations.

He ordered his bill. There was still five minutes to go before contact was lost, but by the time the shuffling waiter had got round to bringing it, he would be able to leave. An hour wasted, but not a moment more.

He paid with a fifty-mark note. The waiter brought his change; two tens, a twenty and some coins. The twenty-mark note had a peculiar jagged tear in the top corner.

The little man swore under his breath. Why did they always have to play games with him? He called the waiter back.

"The dog has been eating this," he said angrily, handing it back to the man.

Any spectator would have thought it a lot of fuss about nothing. In practice it was the recognition procedure. The waiter apologetically handed over another twenty note which was folded in two, and then shuffled away. The little man removed the slip of paper from inside the fold and read it quickly. Then he screwed it up into a little ball and put it in his pocket.

So they had circulated a description of him, had they? They must have traced that lorry driver. The new instructions were to lie low for a week and then come over. The crossing places were being watched for him, so it would have to be by an emergency route.

He stood up and looked round carefully. He was about to make for the door when he saw them. They were seated at a table by the window, engaged in deep conversation, but one of them had looked away just that little bit too slowly. The little man knew at once why they were there. It was something about the clothes, the studied earnestness of the conversation. . . . The warning had been well timed—if it wasn't already too late.

He turned without appearing to have noticed and coolly went towards the door marked *Herren*. On the way through, he caught a glimpse of their reflections in the glass door-panel. They had stopped talking and were watching him.

Inside, he quickly locked himself in one of the cubicles and flushed away the crumpled note from his pocket. Then, looking above him he saw a little frosted glass window. By standing on the lavatory seat he could just reach it, and with an effort, he opened it. It would be a difficult climb, and there was no saying what was on the other side. Besides, he was no athlete. Only a few moments and one of them would come after him if he didn't reappear.

He reopened the cubicle door and had more or less decided to bluff it out when he saw the cupboard. It was a fairly large thing filled with cleaning materials, brushes, pails and a small step ladder. He dragged the ladder out and shoved it into the cubicle he had just left. There was a chance. . . .

He left it there and climbed into the cupboard. It was a tight fit even for him and he had to bend double. As he pulled the door shut behind him, he heard footsteps outside. He froze and unfortunately the cupboard door failed to catch behind him but swung open again. Anyone who was looking could hardly fail to see him.

One of the men came into the room, saw the steps and the open window and drew the obvious conclusion. He didn't look further round the little room. There was a shout and a door banged. A moment or so later both men appeared, talking loudly in English. By this time, the little man had developed cramp in one of his legs. They must see him this time. He couldn't bear the pain much longer. It would be a relief. . . .

"Outside! Get round the back while I pick up the waiter." He heard one shout. The door banged again and there was silence.

The little man forced himself to wait a few moments before scrambling out. He nearly fell as the circulation returned to his leg. Quickly and painfully he pulled out of the cupboard a pair of white overalls that were hanging there, and slipped into them. They were much too big, like another pair he had recently worn, so he had to roll up the bottoms of the trouser legs. Then seizing a bucket and brush, he pushed open the door and brazenly entered the restaurant again.

A crowd had gathered at the far end of the room. The

waiter seemed to be shouting, and above the other heads he could see a policeman's peaked cap. He limped towards the door and out into the street. His leg still hurt him but he went as fast as he could. No one paid any attention to the little man in the ill-fitting overalls as he walked quickly away.

It was beginning to snow again. As he crossed the road, a taxi nearly hit him and a policeman directing the traffic shouted something rude. He had a momentary feeling of fear and then he heard the noise and the sirens. The policeman had other things to think about than jay-walkers. The centre of the demonstration seemed to be just a hundred yards or so ahead. A few laughing groups of students ran past him. They had obviously just left the fun. That was all most of them were protesting for.

Westminster, Thursday Evening

In the room, the only light was coming from the lamp with the green glass shade. The Minister stood up as the Director entered.

"Good evening, Director."

"Good evening, Minister. Cold outside." The visitor couldn't make out the Minister's face very clearly. His eyes hadn't yet grown accustomed to the gloom.

"Nice of you to come—at such short notice too." The Minister's voice was level and controlled, and the Director read the danger signals. He mentally ran over in his mind, as he had been doing since he received the message that the Minister wanted to see him, what the trouble could be. It could only be trouble.

"Do sit down. I thought it better that we talk here. Less likelihood of our being disturbed than at the Ministry. How are things? Everything going O.K.?" The Minister's northern accent betrayed no emotion. The Director was now thoroughly worried. The Minister never indulged in small-talk.

"Not too well, as you know from the reports, Minister. We've been losing a lot of people recently, and by no means all of them are involved in Sonntag. It's extremely worrying."

The Minister played it slow. He had to go carefully with people like the Director. Ministers came and went, but senior State servants like this man had a habit of going on for ever. With their public school and Oxbridge backgrounds, they seemed to be everywhere, and though the Minister felt supremely confident of his ability to put them in their place, intellectually as well as in other ways, his miner's-son background showed through from time to time. He had to make a decision and make it quickly, before they had time to get organized, perhaps get at the P.M. behind his back again, and put his authority aside.

The two men faced each other in the green light. Both very different, both knowing and not knowing the other's worth.

"Yes, I realize that. Very trying. And no success in tracing the culprit, I suppose?"

"Not as yet."

"And the Sonntag thing . . ." The Minister introduced the subject cautiously. "All work on that has stopped, and will stay that way, I hope?"

". . . er . . . yes of course, Minister. You gave your instructions to Armstrong . . ." The Director hesitated slightly, a warning light going on somewhere inside his brain.

"Of course, of course, so I did—to young Armstrong. A good chap that?"

"Among the best we've got, Minister."

"Of course. Very able, and . . . reliable . . ."

The Director waited for the Minister to carry on. He felt very cold and calm now. It was something to do with Sonntag, but the Minister couldn't have got hold of any of the day-to-day stuff on that affair. If he had . . .

"So all work has stopped on the Sonntag thing. I gave my instructions. . . ." The Minister stood up slowly, and, reaching for a single piece of paper which was lying in front of him, stretched forward and handed it to the other man. "Then what, precisely what, is this about, would you mind telling me, Mr Director?" He stressed the "Mr" sarcastically.

It was a typewritten letter purporting to come from one of the Minister's constituents. It had, however, no address. The typing was messy and inaccurate but the message was clear enough. It talked about a girl, a Miss Weinberg, having been recruited to undertake a certain task. The word "Sonntag" appeared several times in the text. There were some inaccuracies in the story it told, but basically it was correct. It passed through the Director's mind that this particular leak might cause more harm than all the ones that had preceded it. Someone, somewhere had been very clever, and had not only known the facts of the case—he could see at a glance that the inaccuracies were deliberate, but subtle enough to deceive the Minister—but also, that the same person knew the Minister and his predilections. So the other side—if it was the other side—had started playing British politics, so to speak.

When he looked up from the letter, the Minister's back was turned to him, but the shoulders were shaking, and that said a great deal.

"May I try to explain . . . ?"

"You may try, Director. But to me, unless it's an absolute denial that everything that is said in the letter is untrue, it looks like a complete and far-reaching disobedience of a Ministerial order. Don't you agree?"

The Director began to explain, but from the outset, he realized it was hopeless. The Minister had been given the weapon which, subconsciously, he had been seeking for years, a weapon to hit at the whole organization. He had always disliked it, all it did, and all it stood for. It was dishonest, underhand, and if such things were on occasions permissible, then it was only in time of war. He wouldn't begin to be convinced now of the need for constant readiness, and a proper flow of information. To him the "security of the State" was suspect ground for any action in Government.

The Director stated that it wasn't a deliberate contravention of the Minister's wishes. The girl had more or less appeared unasked; and it had seemed to Armstrong, indeed to the organization, to him, that she had presented an excellent opportunity for getting at the facts. She could, if discovered, plead that she was looking for the background to her fiancé's . . .

"And didn't it occur to you, to any of you, that you were using, going to use the better feelings of a perfectly innocent girl to further your own—the aims of your whole organization?"

"But she would be doing that in any case. It was she who had started to follow . . ."

"And didn't you think of trying to dissuade her? Perhaps you did, until you saw the benefit of using an unthinking, unknowing, semi-Civil Servant." The Minister spat the words out. He still did not turn to look at the other man.

"If I may continue . . ." The Director could also get annoyed.

"Of course."

"She was—is—hell bent on finding the truth. She probably won't, but there is no danger to us."

"That sums up your whole attitude: no danger to us. Quite apart from any human feelings involved, I've also heard this from you before. That's what you said at the beginning about the whole Sonntag thing. It was fool-proof—wasn't that your word for it? Now look at it. Who's right, you or me? Tell me that. I've said it before—you people have no feelings. You don't care. Individuals are just names on paper to you. In my view you and Armstrong typify this attitude."

"But, Minister . . ."

The Minister turned round, and drew himself up to the fullness of his sturdy height and said coldly: "I consider this whole affair to be in direct opposition to the instructions which, I, as a Minister of the Crown, gave to Armstrong in this very room. I have therefore no

alternative but to inform the Prime Minister and to
ask him . . ."

"I do not intend to be accused of duplicity by you or
any man." The Director no longer spoke as a Civil
Servant to his Minister. "I acted in very good faith, and
in accordance with the responsibility I have. I therefore . . ."

"What faith? What responsibility?" The Minister
had by now reached the peak of one of his well-known
rages, "You have . . ."

"I therefore have no alternative," the Director went
on, cold, white and erect, "but to offer my resignation,
since you have obviously no further trust in my ability
to manage my Department."

"I accept it, Mr Director, indeed I do."

TEN

Düsseldorf, Friday Evening

As soon as he came into the room, she realized something was wrong. By then they had begun to trust each other enough, and she had stopped using him as a sparring partner. In return, he had given her as much of the background to Sonntag as was necessary for her purpose. He had deliberately not gone too far, for her own protection, in case she got picked up. She couldn't spill anything she didn't know about.

"Anything turn up?"

"Not so far. But I can't go on just sitting here waiting. I used the contact you suggested, and told a little of what I was after, but I've heard nothing further."

"Well, that's all to the good, I suppose." He took off his coat.

She looked at him curiously for a moment, and then went on: "I've decided to go over tomorrow. I've made all the necessary preparations—all I think necessary, that is. I'd be glad of your views—and approval of course," she added as an afterthought. "Not your assistance, though. If I'm playing the maiden in distress, then I'd better play it my way, without help. You said yourself that one could never be sure where the leak was. It may be too late. They may know I've been on to you already. I thought this had better be our last contact."

Armstrong thought momentarily that it wasn't a bad

thing that it was all over. She was showing too great an aptitude. She seemed to be taking over. She had certainly learned the vocabulary quickly.

"It's not going to be like that, I'm afraid. Everything has gone wrong."

"What's happened?"

He showed her the cable he had just decoded. She read it slowly. "As you see, I've to go back, and I've to take you—you've to come with me."

"And if I don't choose . . . ?"

"We've had that out already."

"So we have. I forgot." She smiled quickly at him, and it worried him for a moment.

Then she said: "How about that drink? You never did get me one that day."

He ignored her, and went on: "I'm sorry about this. Something serious is going on. They're falling like ninepins at the top. The Minister's had it in for us for a long time."

"And I'm the sword, so to speak. It's me that should be sorry."

"It wasn't your choosing."

"Oh well," she sighed, "it can't be helped . . . We'd . . . I'd probably not have got anywhere in any case."

He looked at her sharply. She was still smiling. It wasn't in character, and he nearly asked her what she was thinking. But somehow he didn't.

"That drink?"

It was inevitable, she supposed. Not that it worried her. There always had been an attraction of opposites.

There was a soullessness about the flat Captain Hermes had provided Armstrong with. A senior-staff appartment, was how he had described it. The furniture was there, of the post-war plywood variety, but the trappings were lacking. There were faded marks on the wallpaper where the previous tenant had removed his pictures. The bookshelves were empty. But there was a kitchen, and that gave more independence than a hotel.

The chairs in front of the electric fire which was turned on for colour despite the central heating; the table, two glasses, the whisky bottle, the cracked saucer with melting ice cubes floating in it: she would remember it with a certain sympathy.

He impressed her with the obvious monasticism of his way of life. Of a type she had met only rarely. There had been a trace of it in Alex. Perhaps they selected them that way. She could understand why. It was almost appealing enough in itself to spark off the feeling within her. Like a man felt with a pretty nun.

They stood up together, and he switched off the fire. They hadn't discussed it, but it was as if they had, and there had been no argument, only agreement.

She moved over to him, almost making the running. But the response was there. The black corduroy tunic-dress fell away, and she stood in the simple white shirt—almost like a man's—that she wore underneath. Like a nightdress, with her long legs, slightly parted, hips thrust a little forward—immensely provocative.

He came round behind her, very close, and his arms folded round her waist. She put her head back and her hair fell into his eyes. His large fingers fumbled clumsily with the shirt buttons, so she helped him, and then breaking free ran into the bedroom.

He went through slowly after her, unembarrassed that his excitement would be obvious to her. She was standing naked by the bed, with the same stance, the same thrust of the hips. Again she came over to him. Neither of them spoke. This time she helped him with his shirt, her fingers playing lightly and sensuously across his chest.

Till that moment it was as if she had been seducing him. Then he took over. The uncomfortable bed was no inconvenience. What it lacked in softness, it made up for in size. He pursued her nakedness across it and trapped her against the padded headboard. She felt completely, gloriously crushed, as he weighed down on her. Moaning gently, her finger-nails dug strongly into the muscles of his back.

Some time during the night, reality came briefly back to them, and they lay awake, side by side, talking quietly. After a while they made love again, but more gently this time. Then they slept.

Düsseldorf, Saturday Morning

A brief wintry sun came in through the slats of the blind over the windows. As he woke, she was standing at the end of the bed, wrapped in his dressing-gown.

"You've run out of milk."

He smiled. "Breakfast? That would be nice. I take my coffee black, and I haven't had cereals since I was a child."

"I can't stand black coffee. It introduces me to the day too quickly. I'll go out and get some milk; I saw a shop at the corner."

He made a face. Then he sat up in the bed, hands behind his head, and watched her dress. She brushed her hair for quite a long time.

"I won't be too long. The kettle's on." She picked up her bag, blew him a kiss and went out. He turned on his side, and dozed off, more contented than he had felt for a very long time.

The telephone woke him. He looked at his watch. Almost an hour had gone by. He couldn't hear any movement in the flat, and he felt a moment of panic.

It was Hermes, asking when he was leaving. He had his ticket. "Both tickets?" he asked. He almost knew the answer before it came. She had left a message that she wouldn't require it.

"You must stop her."

"Take too long. You had the restriction on her lifted. The passport control officers will have taken her name off the list. Sorry."

"See what you can do. It's very important."

"I'll try." Hermes sounded amused. "But don't rely on it."

Armstrong put the phone down, and went into the kitchen. The table was set for one. A carton of milk was unopened on the table.

ELEVEN

Berlin, Saturday Afternoon

Lance-Corporal Hennik drove slowly along Kleiststrasse towards the Kaiser Wilhelm Platz in the big green Humber which carried the Berlin Garrison signs on its wings. He had just taken a lieutenant-colonel to Tempelhof Airport, and the officer had dismissed him early, so he had plenty of time before he was due back at his unit by the Olympic Stadium. He could drop in the letter on the way. It had only arrived with that morning's delivery, so, they could hardly complain, as they had done in the past, that he was a bit slow in passing the letters on.

Hennik was certainly a very minor traitor. If he ever were brought to task for his crime, he would laugh at the term. All he did was to receive letters and the occasional package through the British Forces Post Office, and if they were from this mad Aunt Agnes woman, he knew he had to take them to the house in Charlottenburg. At fifty marks a time, who would have turned it down? As a member of transport section, he could even do it in Army time. This was hardly being a traitor.

And were he ever questioned about his unofficial postal activities, and asked how it all began, he would say, quite simply, that it was because someone had asked him to do it. Nothing much wrong with that. The man had helped him out of a spot after all.

It had been one evening, fairly early on in his tour in

Berlin. He had left his barrack-room colleagues drinking in the N.A.A.F.I. Club, and had walked the long road down to the Kurfürstendamm, past all the neon lights of the island-city. He liked the lights. Before enlisting, almost the only neon light he remembered had been in the window of the little store in the village where he had been brought up. Yes, he liked lights.

In some clip-joint behind the big *Ka De We* store, he had hesitantly ordered a beer from the girl behind the bar. He couldn't speak a word of German, but beer is an international word.

He was told that beer was out. Either a whisky at an exorbitant price, or a very expensive bottle of German champagne. He reluctantly bought a whisky, vaguely aware that he was being got at. He took it to a table, and immediately a girl came up to him. Would he buy her a drink too? The old bait, and he swallowed it.

Later, of course, he hadn't enough to pay the bill. They threatened that the police would be called. He looked round for the door, thinking perhaps of making a dash for it. But there were these two big fellows, and he didn't fancy both a punch-up and the police as well.

Then this little chap sitting at a nearby table came up and told the bouncers to relax. He spoke to them quickly in a low voice, and some money changed hands. The little man came and sat beside him. The girl who had been sitting with him seemed to have disappeared.

"Call me Hermann," the little man had said. Funny, pernickety little chap. A big breath of wind, and he looked as if he would be blown away. Anyway, he had said something about not liking Tommies being bullied. Not their fault that they were in Berlin. Defending it against the Red Menace or something. Berliners should be grateful and not try to catch them out. "Right?" . . . "Right," he had replied.

So Hermann paid his bill. No, it wasn't much. Yes, they did pay one badly in the army. How long had Lance-Corporal Hennik been in Berlin? Many friends? No? That was a pity. The stranger bought him a drink, and then another. Hennik was more used to beer than to whisky.

Later the man, Hermann, had told him about this old aunt of his in London, who didn't trust the ordinary postal services. Funny what old people were like, but things did get lost so easily. Besides, it cost a lot to send airmail letters to Germany. Didn't the army have their own postal service? So he had guessed rightly. Then supposing Hermann's Aunt Agnes were to write through the army post office, care of him, could he pass the letters on? . . . Couldn't refuse to oblige a man who had got him out of a very tricky situation.

Lance-Corporal Hennik didn't remember much more about the evening thereafter, until of course, they had shown him the photographs. But that was a few weeks later. It was after he had seen the army circular about penalties for misuse of army postal channels. By that time, too, Aunt Agnes was being pretty prolific in her letter-writing and had taken to sending small packets as well, for onward transmission. All a bit much to ask.

So Hennik had gone to the old bullet-scarred house in Charlottenburg, where he used to leave the letters with the old man in the basement flat, and told him to tell

Hermann that he couldn't act as postman any more. He had left feeling much happier, but it didn't last long.

Another man, whom he hadn't seen before, had come up to Hennik the next night as he was coming out of the N.A.A.F.I. He thought at first he was drunk and had tried to get away. But the man was persistent. He had a message, he said, from Hennik's friend, Hermann, who was upset at the fact that Hennik had stopped being helpful. It was such a pity. Wouldn't Hennik change his mind? But Hennik was firm. Enough was enough.

Then the man had produced the photographs, and had given Hennik some copies to take away with him. But he kept the negatives. They were curious photographs. They showed Hennik himself, in an unusual state, and there seemed to be these two women. He could vaguely remember something. . . .

Not something Hennik's mother would like to see, would she, the man had said. Might give her quite a turn. Hennik remembered having talked to Hermann about his frail old mother, with her strong Puritanism and her weak heart. He was deeply shocked at the thought. But he was also frightened and agreed to carry on. The man had thrown in the "fifty-marks-a-time" offer for good measure.

Hennik wasn't clever. He knew that. But he did have the ability of dismissing unpleasant things from his mind. So were he asked about his postal activities, somehow the photographs wouldn't be mentioned. He just did it because someone had done him a favour. Nothing wrong with that, was there?

As the weeks had passed, it didn't seem so bad in any

case. He acted automatically now. He had helped himself forget by secretly burning the photographs and then flushing the ash away down a drain. The letters and packets were very frequent now. Aunt Agnes and Hermann were right. No one ever bothered to open them. Who would look for someone smuggling something *out* of Britain, to a soldier. It was only the inward parcels that the Customs checked. . . . Funny that Aunt Agnes was so clever, since she was obviously a bit mad. Hennik knew because he had opened one of her letters once out of curiosity, and then stuck it up again. It was mainly a lot of jibberish, full of funny numbers, like a football pools form.

Lance-Corporal Hennik drove carefully north-east along Kantstrasse, and then turned right along a narrow road towards the disused canal. He pulled into a parking-lot a few hundred metres from the house. They had warned him not to park right outside just in case.

He walked slowly along the road. There was still plenty of time. He stopped at the house and went down the worn outside steps to the cellar flat. He hadn't time to knock before the door opened. It was the little man who had paid his drink bill for him. Hennik felt a shiver of apprehension run through him.

"Good afternoon, Corporal. I came specially to see you. You've been a bit long in coming though."

"I had to take an officer to Tempelhof. I couldn't get here before." God, they were ungrateful.

"O.K. But come in. Have you the letter?"

Hennik handed it over. "It just arrived this morning."

"Good, Good. You do your best." The little man appeared mollified. They went into the dowdy living-room. The old man was nowhere to be seen.

"Now we have a further favour to ask you, Corporal. Nothing much, and not worth worrying about."

Hennik's pulse quickened. He said nothing but looked surly.

"We'd like to borrow your car—yes, your army one, the official one, that is."

"But that's not possible. I can't do that. They'd find out at once."

"Everything is possible. It will only be for a couple of hours. You'll wait here while we're using it. You can easily make up an imaginary detail, I'm sure. We'll help you there. A phone call from one of our other, er, con-tacts will do the trick. You leave that to us."

"But it's too dangerous. I'd get—I can't!"

"You can, you know."

"No, it's gone too far . . ."

"Aren't you forgetting something, Corporal?" The little man waved some photographs in Hennik's face. The soldier didn't even look at them. He went very pale. No hero and a very minor traitor.

Confused and unhappy, he left the house in Charlot-tenburg a few moments later. He had agreed to come back with his car in five days' time.

"Four o'clock precisely. Leave your cover to us." That's what the man had said.

Perhaps it was fortunate for Lance-Corporal Hennik that he was able to share his worries without much delay. As he came round the corner to the parking-place, he was aware of two men in gaberdine coats standing beside his car. He didn't pay them much attention. He had his own worries, and the only thing that would have jolted him out of his thoughts would have been if they had been wearing the red caps of the Military Police.

He unlocked the car door and started to get in. One of the men came up to him and said in English: "Lance-Corporal Hennik?"

"Yes?" he answered blankly.

"O.K. Get in the back. You're under arrest. Sergeant Wheeler of Special Investigation Branch. This is Lieutenant Bambridge, Intelligence Corps. Corporal! Take that stupid look off your face. You haven't forgotten how to salute an officer, have you?"

Only a few miles to the east, an attractive, dark-haired girl had just passed through the Allied "Checkpoint Charlie", and was busy explaining the reasons for her arrival in the German Democratic Republic to the Sector Control. She had her press card and the entry permit which she had been given earlier.

Had she been more used to the game, she might have been worried by the ease with which she was allowed through, and by why she wasn't being asked many more searching questions about the paper she was writing for, and what her political leanings were.

She might just have also noticed the large Russian-built car in which two men were sitting, over on the other side of the barbed-wire fence. But she was so relieved at getting through so easily that she walked quickly past without looking around her.

Inside the car, the man in the passenger seat said quietly: "That's the one."

The driver made to get out of the car, but the other man put a hand on his arm. "No, wait! Leave her strictly alone for the moment. D'you understand? We'll get the others only if we leave her to it. Keep her strictly in view, though. She's pretty. The men should enjoy their work for once."

TWELVE

Whitehall, Monday Morning

Armstrong sat at his empty desk and gazed vacantly out of the window. Not that he could see much. The net curtains were hardly necessary, since the windows hadn't been washed for months. The Ministry of Public Buildings and Works didn't have this particular office on their lists, and arrangements for window-cleaning were left to the whims of the one-armed ex-sergeant-major who acted as janitor.

The desk was empty. He hadn't asked the registry to pass up to him the pile of work that he knew would have been building up for him while he had been away. He had to think. The paper would clog his mind if he started to work through it.

She had gone across, he was sure of that. They probably knew that she was there if they hadn't already picked her up. He tried to think impersonally of an agent potentially lost. This time it didn't work.

He asked himself the usual questions. Whom did she know? Whom could she incriminate? Had they found her out? What would they do with her if they did have her? Then the inevitable last question. What could be done about it?

Working on the assumption that they were on to her, he tried finding some of the answers. They came slowly.

She didn't know much. He had seen to that. But she did have some contacts, otherwise she wouldn't have got anywhere. Did this matter, he wondered, if the next question had the response he thought it had—that someone in the centre of the organization was spilling the beans? If this was the case, the other side knew a lot more than the girl. And she had just added herself to the pile they would mop up when it suited them.

He could see it now. They had them all, or most of the agents at least. But they would wait, put a tail on every one of them, just in case anything further came up. That's how it always was when a network was broken open. Don't rush. Wait till everyone possible is exposed, and then—the quick kill.

The last question on the check list: what could be done about it? On the face of it, very little—except find the leak, of course.

Armstrong drew a piece of writing-paper from the top drawer of his desk. He took out his pen and began, slowly and carefully, to write down a list of names. Lists of names were rare in the organization. They were too dangerous, too insecure. People should never be linked together on lists. But this was different. Who had known about Sonntag, who knew enough to have prompted his kidnapping at the Curtain? Who would also have thought of writing to the Minister?

He was half-way through when the door opened and the Director came in.

"Morning, Paul!" he said breezily. "I've come to say goodbye."

"I'm sorry about . . ." Armstrong began.

The Director brushed the remark aside. "Don't let's talk about it. Time a new brush was applied, I have no doubt, and a new artist behind it." He sat down casually in a chair as if he hadn't a care in the world. In one way he hadn't.

"If there *is* a new artist, and we don't all end up on the dole," Armstrong responded.

"Oh, there is no fear of that. The Minister is a rare beast, and there are others in the Cabinet who have their heads screwed on. He has unscrewed my head, and my guess is that that is as far as he'll be allowed to go. My only worry, and here I'm speaking confidentially, is that inside the organization, the brighter people won't get to the top as a result of this fracas, at least not for quite some time. We'll get some good devoted—no, I am being too indiscreet. You might begin thinking I'm bitter, which I'm not."

Armstrong knew he was being told that the future for him was not too bright. He had been closely involved with Sonntag, and those who didn't like it and him would see that he was put in his place. He had half realized this for himself, but he was grateful to the Director for bringing it home to him.

"Oh, I don't know, Sir. But it will be hard to follow your footsteps."

"Rubbish. But this is no time for chatter. I've got to go and shake a few more hands." The Director stood up, stretched himself and began to move towards the door. Then he spotted the list on Armstrong's desk. He stopped.

"I know I'm about to leave, Paul, but I must say, I'm surprised. You know the rules." He looked sharply at the younger man.

"Sometimes it is necessary to clarify one's mind, Sir. This is perhaps one of those occasions." Armstrong stiffened slightly as he spoke.

"You know," the Director said, seating himself once again in a chair ". . . why I spotted that list, Paul, why I thought it odd without even looking at the names on it? It might well have been an invitation list to a cocktail party you were going to give, mightn't it? But I knew at once it wasn't. Do you know why? Because," he went on, without waiting for an answer, "I've just been compiling a similar list. But then I tore it up. I'm leaving after all. It would just have been a frustrating intellectual exercise. I would never have known the answer. So I tore it up. I don't like to leave with a question mark in my pocket. May I see?"

Armstrong handed it over silently.

The other man worked his way down the list carefully as if digesting each name in turn. It was two or three minutes before anything happened. Armstrong sat and watched him.

At length the Director took a little gold propelling pencil from his inside pocket and wrote something on the paper. Then he stood up and handed it back to Armstrong.

"Well, you've got all the important ones on it. Almost my own list. No, don't bother reading it now. I must be off. I've a lot to do. Goodbye Paul. It's been a pleasure. We must have dinner together sometime. . . ." It was one of those vague invitations, but the handshake was firm and definite.

When he had gone, Armstrong sat down at the desk again, and looked at his list. Against one of the names was a faint pencilled cross. Another name had been added at the bottom. It too had a cross against it. Then there was something else scribbled in the margin. It read: "Where's your own name?"

Why the crosses? Did the Director know or was it merely a suspicion? Why couldn't he have explained? Was it because he didn't want to blacken a name without proof? Presumably. Armstrong took it so on trust.

After some time, he rang for the clerk and had his papers brought to him. He had guessed correctly. There was quite a pile of work. Determinedly, he began to go through the files. It took him most of the day. He didn't even stop for lunch, but sent the janitor across the road to the pub, to buy sandwiches and a bottle of beer. It was seven-thirty in the evening when he stopped. He picked up the remaining files, and went out of the room, locking the door behind him.

The building was more or less deserted, and the only light came from behind the big steel door of the registry, where the duty clerk was waiting to lock up.

"All right, Jones. You needn't wait. I'll lock up. I'm so far behind with having been away, and I must catch up. You have changed the combination on the door lock, have you? O.K., then I'll slam the door behind me when I'm through."

When the clerk had left, Armstrong partly shut the

steel door, wedging it with a broken chair leg so that it wouldn't slam and lock him in. It would also serve to give him some slight warning if anyone were to come in unexpectedly and disturb him.

He carefully spread some of his own papers and files over the clerk's desk, to give the appearance of working on them there. Then he went across to the grey steel filing cabinets which lined the far side of the room. They held the working papers belonging to his colleagues, and there were names on the doors indicating to whom the contents belonged. The cabinets weren't locked. The security people reckoned that the combination locks on the door, the steel shutters over the windows, plus an elaborate alarm system and the resident guards, were enough protection for the contents.

He opened one cabinet. Its shelves held files and some desk-trays filled with current papers. He sheafed through them carefully. Most of the files were on routine, unimportant matters. There were a couple of large sealed envelopes in one of the trays. He would have liked to look inside, but he couldn't risk that for the moment.

Reports, pamphlets, letters. The junk of any office. Then, down at the bottom of another tray, a photostat of a telegram. It was a scruffy piece of paper, and it had been folded and re-folded several times. He opened it carefully. At once he recognized the message he had sent from Germany.

Odd that he should find a copy of it in that particular tray. Telegrams like that went to the separate administration registry. Odd too, perhaps, that it should be so scruffy and folded, as if it had been in someone's pocket.

Yes, there was a tiny piece of fluff caught in a tear in the paper. He felt the excitement of a detective.

Armstrong placed the telegram back precisely where he had found it. He looked through the rest of the cabinet, but found nothing else of significance. He shut it and went across to another cabinet in the corner of the room. He had just opened it and had briefly seen a pair of women's shoes sitting on a shelf inside, when he heard a sound in the corridor outside the registry. He shut the door quickly and turned towards his papers on the desk.

The piece of wood was scraped aside, and Brander came into the room.

The words came too quickly, and he blurted out: "Hello, Brander. Just clearing up a backlog of work. Sorry about that bit of wood. I didn't want to get locked in."

As soon as he had spoken, he realized that he need not have started to explain. Brander, after showing some slight surprise at seeing him sitting there instead of the duty clerk, barely nodded to him. His mind was obviously elsewhere as he walked across to his own particular filing cabinet.

Armstrong watched him out of the corner of his eye, curiously. He saw the other man open the cupboard, take out a large sealed envelope, and place it in the brief-case he was carrying. Somehow, Armstrong thought, the action was inevitable. Then Brander looked up almost guiltily and caught Armstrong looking.

"Working late, eh?" Brander asked, with a smile that might have been trying to be pleasant. Armstrong might as well not have bothered with explaining his presence there.

"So am I," Brander went on, without waiting for a response. "Lots to do with the Director gone. How was Germany? Not so good, I hear."

Armstrong said something formal in reply, which again, Brander seemed not to hear.

"Well, I must away! Good night, Armstrong, good night." The older man left the room, leaving Armstrong wondering a little at his uncharacteristic haste.

The next hour was spent in fruitless search. Nothing to go on, or was there? On an impulse, Armstrong went back to the first cabinet he had opened, and took out the one remaining large sealed envelope. Then he went across to the steel door of the registry and deliberately slammed it shut. He picked up the internal phone, and got on to the resident guard.

"It's Armstrong here. I'm afraid I've locked myself in the registry. Can you get the duty clerk on the phone, and ask him to come along and unlock me. Tell him I'm very sorry to disturb him. There's no hurry, though. I've got plenty of work to keep me occupied." He put the receiver down.

Taking the electric kettle that the clerks used to brew their tea, he plugged it in, and waited for it to boil. Then he took the envelope and examined it carefully. The top flap was well sealed, but the bottom one looked more promising. He remembered his instructor during training telling him that the bottom flap was less likely to be noticed.

He held the envelope over the steam coming from the spout of the kettle, and, using a paper knife, eased the flap apart. Then he turned the kettle off, and took the contents from the envelope. Before looking at them, he placed the envelope to dry between two heavy books. It was less likely to warp that way.

It was a large cypher book of the variety that consisted of lists of numbers that could only be used once. A message could be deciphered only if one had a copy of the book, and there were only two copies. This particular book had already been used for sending cyphered messages, since the numbers in it had been crossed off.

He felt disappointment at his find. He had locked himself in for nothing, and he was getting hungry.

Then he found the cable. It was inside the cover of the code book. It was a long report from the Berlin Station about a security breach by a British soldier. Something a Head of Security should rightly know about. But why seal it up in an envelope with a used code book? It was the only copy of the cable too. "No copies to be made," Brander had written in the corner. Armstrong recognized the writing.

That meant that no one else at the London end would have seen it. No copies were made when a cable was too unimportant to bother people with, or it was very important and needed restricted distribution.

He looked at his watch. He still had plenty of time. The duty clerk lived in North London somewhere and wouldn't hurry. Armstrong could imagine himself being cursed for locking himself in. The clerk would keep him waiting to teach him a lesson.

He switched on the registry photostat machine and

started copying the cypher book, page by page. There were a hundred and fifty pages and it took him some time. When he had finished, he placed the code book and the cable back in the envelope and re-sealed the bottom flap. He was quite pleased with his work. It looked almost untampered with, but for good measure he deliberately upset a bottle of ink over it. The bottle had been standing without a cap on the cupboard shelf beside the place where the envelope had been lying. Brander would assume that in his hurry, he had done it himself when he had removed the other envelope. It would also teach him not to leave the tops off ink bottles in future.

Then he drafted a cable to the Berlin Station, asking for more background to the soldier case. He asked that the reply be sent personal to him alone. He also asked for a copy of the numbers in the letter they had found on the soldier. Berlin's telegram had said that they guessed that code was of the "one-time" variety that couldn't normally be broken. But could they send the figures, nonetheless?

As he finished drafting, Armstrong heard the sound of someone working at the combination lock outside the registry. He put the cable in his pocket, and picked up one of his files.

THIRTEEN

Kennington, Tuesday Morning

A bell rang incessantly beside him. He pulled a pillow over his ear, but it went on ringing. Automatically he stretched out a hand in the dark and picked up the receiver. The ringing stopped.

"Herr, sorry, Mr Armstrong, please?"

"Speaking," he replied. "Who's there?"

"This is Tesco, you remember me. Walt Tesco."

"Who? Oh, yes, I remember. The journalist, that it?"

"That's right, Mr Armstrong. I wonder if I could come and see you."

Armstrong switched on the bed-side light and looked at his watch.

"Do you know what time it is, Herr Tesco? I'll tell you. It's three-thirty in the morning and I'm very tired. Call back in the morning will you."

"But it's urgent. I'm sorry it's so late. The overnight plane got delayed, and I've just managed to get to a phone."

"What's all this about? You mean you're in London?"

"Yes, I've come to see you. Can I come round? I have a message," Tesco repeated.

"What message? From whom?"

"If you don't mind me saying so, Mr Armstrong, you are being a bit slow. You don't want me to talk on the phone do you?"

"Sorry, sorry. I had a hard night. O.K., come round," Armstrong said reluctantly.

"I'll be with you in half an hour." The phone went dead.

Armstrong woke up properly then. He had indeed had a hard night. After getting the cable off, he had gone to his club for dinner, and then had deliberately drowned his cares till about two hours ago. The hangover hadn't even had time to set in.

He went through to the bathroom and got the Alka Selzer. His head was throbbing. He put on a kettle for some coffee. As he lit the gas he suddenly realized that it was strange that Tesco had known his telephone number and his address.

At four o'clock precisely, Tesco arrived. He looked as fresh and fit as he ever would.

Armstrong, who had resolutely remained in his pyjamas and dressing-gown to remind his guest that the night wasn't over, took him into the book-filled living-room.

"Nice place you've got here, Mr Armstrong."

"O.K., thanks. But let's remember the time and cut the pleasantries if you don't mind. What was your call about?"

Tesco looked hurt and Armstrong relented a little. "Have some coffee?"

"Thanks—you don't have anything stronger, do you?"

Armstrong winced at the thought, but produced a bottle of whisky and two glasses. He poured himself one as well, and immediately felt a bit better. He had drunk himself sober again, he hoped.

"I got the message this, or should I say yesterday, morning," Tesco began. "It worried me stiff at first. But then as the instructions were to pass it on to you—to the side of the gods, so to speak—I thought, what the hell. It's from her, of course," he added, almost as an afterthought.

"You mean that you came specially over here because you got a message to pass on to me?" Armstrong asked incredulously.

"That's it. You see, I suppose that I always have the sneaking hope that one day there will be a story in it for me. Besides, I did once promise Miss Weinberg that I would help her any time I could. She's a fine girl." Tesco allowed himself a slight sigh.

"Where's the message?" Tesco pulled a wad of airmail paper from his pocket. "It's not all this," he said, smiling. "As you'll see, it's buried in the middle of the text of an article I'm writing. Less chance of anyone finding it that way, don't you think? The message itself begins at the bottom of the second page."

Armstrong marvelled briefly at Tesco's professionalism. Yet another spy *manqué*. Then he began to read.

Jo had got across with surprisingly little difficulty and had gone straight to Leipzig. She had explained to enquirers that she was reporting on the current annual industrial fair.

On arrival, she got straight on to one of the contacts and had given him the story of her fiancé having been murdered. She had his sympathy, and with his help, she had managed to trace Alex's movements.

The last evening that Alex had been seen alive had been in one of the big restaurants which catered mainly for tourists. It was too expensive for any mere East German. He had had dinner with one or two foreign businessmen who were preparing for the Leipzig Fair. As cover, Alex had claimed that this was what he was doing too.

Jo had, with difficulty, traced one of the businessmen, a Japanese buyer, who was still in Leipzig. He had remembered the evening clearly. They had all wondered why Alex hadn't turned up for the fair itself, after all the hard work he had put in. The buyer had been really sorry to hear about his death. The others would be too.

The businessman had told Jo that the dinner was nearly over when Alex had been called away from the table to take a long-distance telephone call from London. After a while, he had returned to the others looking very worried. Something had gone wrong with the display material his firm were sending out, he had explained.

"That was my boss on the phone. She's a woman and she never lets up. Never let a woman boss you, it's hell!"

They had all laughed. Alex had said he had to leave.

"She wants me to get on to our local representative, now, at this time of night!"

They had watched him go out on to the pavement. He had put up his umbrella, since it was raining hard. Then a little man had come up to him and they had spoken together for a few minutes before they both got into a big car that was parked by the kerb just outside the window.

The Japanese businessman remembered that clearly, because someone had remarked how lucky Alex was to have met a friend who would give him a lift. Taxis were so hard to come by in Leipzig these days. Doubtless he would claim it as a taxi ride—on expenses—nonetheless. They had all laughed at that. They knew the expense-account game.

Jo hadn't much else to say in her report. Almost as an appendix to it, she remarked casually that she thought she was being followed. Nothing definite, no actual proof. But just in case, she was sending the report now, via an Austrian journalist who knew Tesco.

She ended up apologizing for the solitary breakfast.

Tesco and Armstrong looked at each other for a moment in silence. Then Armstrong poured out another whisky for them both.

"I didn't get the significance of the last remark," Tesco said.

"No, no, of course not." Armstrong didn't elaborate.

"Now what?" asked Tesco.

"I'll be quite honest with you. I don't know." It didn't seem odd to Armstrong that he was going to take Tesco into his confidence. They were both so different, and had first met as interrogator and prisoner respectively, but it no longer mattered to either of them.

"She's in danger?"

"Of course. She has been since she went over. I'm convinced they know she's there and are watching her to see if she turns anything new up. But my hands are tied."

"Can I help?" Tesco volunteered.

"I can't see . . . Well, maybe . . . Can you get a message back?"

"I could try. I have a lot of friends. Journalists are everywhere. I could even go over myself, I suppose."

"You must be keen to get that story."

"Perhaps . . ."

"O.K. We'll see. But leave it for twenty-four hours. I have a couple of other irons in the fire."

Whitehall, Tuesday Lunchtime

Berlin Station was quick off the mark. It had always paid dividends to have good people there. The reply was waiting for him when he came in.

He nursed a glass of water in his hand as he read it, wishing his headache would slacken off a little. With an effort, he composed a reply. He sent it top priority, and personal for the Head of Station:

"Imperative arrange Corporal to take car to rendezvous as arranged. Hope to arrive personally Berlin Wednesday evening. Please ensure *no one*, repeat *no one* else is informed of this. Will report arrival time later."

Armstrong was taking several risks. First of all that the leak wasn't the Head of Berlin Station himself. That was a minor worry. Armstrong knew him too well.

Second was that the cabled code numbers would reveal something, and that they would be solvable with the cypher book he had photostated. He needed time to try this line. Third, he had to get permission to go. This, in the normal course of events, he wouldn't get. The Director was gone. There was no one else to give it, or who would want to give it. Or was there . . .?

FOURTEEN

Whitehall, Tuesday Afternoon

It was almost ten minutes before Brander moved. He felt the sickness in his stomach which he hadn't felt since he had been caught stealing when he was a schoolboy.

He held the envelope in front of him, staring at it as if transfixed. The inkstains on the outside didn't disguise to him the fact that it had been opened. He was an old campaigner with envelopes, and the hair stuck along the flap was no longer there.

He knew at once it was Armstrong. Plenty of opportunity when he had been locked in. But why had he discovered that there was something to hide inside the envelope? Why had he suspected? Had he somehow been traced through the letter to the Minister? More important—what now?

Brander knew that he had to act, but he felt weak. The wound in his leg throbbed. He had to go out. He had to pass on the word that he was discovered. He felt defeated. What did it matter any more? It had all got out of hand in any case. He was glad it was all over.

But was it? He began to exercise a little control. Hadn't he seen, as Head of Security, how people came too easily to the conclusion that they had been found out? What did Armstrong really have? An old code book and a perfectly legitimate telegram amounted to nothing, certainly nothing in the nature of an indictment. Even if the man did begin to put two and two together, where would it lead him? Not to Brander—at least not for some time. He had time on his side.

Time, time. He must have time. Time to think. Time to get it off his chest. It wouldn't be so bad for him if he turned Queen's Evidence. He wasn't the main culprit. He had come unwillingly into it. He had been blackmailed—yes, that's what he would say. That was true enough, and what else could he have done? Indeed— the idea developed within his mind—he would say that he had deliberately allowed himself to be blackmailed in order to uncover the truth. They would believe him— him, the Head of Security. They *had* to believe him. What was the proof after all?

He began to convince himself. It would work. It would be all right. In fact it would do his career good. Brander, the man who had uncovered the whole affair. He might even get the Director's job.

But the doubt, the fear was still there. It would be no good, if, after his confession, or rather his revelation of the truth, there were those about who might be able to save their own skins by blackening him. That was no good. That wouldn't do. He would have to be the only one left to tell the truth. But how? An ultimatum, that was it. An ultimatum which proposed either there be a defection, a disappearance, or . . . or . . . Brander shuddered. He wasn't a violent man.

Brander took his tweed coat from the peg behind the office door, and, putting the envelope in his briefcase, started to leave the room. Then he stopped. He took a sheet of paper and wrote a note to Armstrong. He suggested that there was something in the envelope that might be of interest. Then he put the note and the envelope in a yet larger envelope, sealed it and went out into the corridor and along to the registry.

He handed the envelope to the clerk on duty.

"Give this to Mr Armstrong if I'm not back by this evening," he said. "Not before though."

The clerk took note. Such requests were not uncommon in the organization.

Outside, the morning shopping crowds tired him quickly, and he called a taxi. He sat well back in the passenger seat and felt more confident. What he was going to do, he had to do, in the name of duty.

It was one of those faceless blocks of service flats that seemed to have been dumped rather than built all over that part of South Kensington. He paid the taxi off at the corner of the street, and then walked round the corner to the side entrance of the building. As he entered he looked round instinctively. There was no one in sight except a large fat foreign-looking man, with a camera round his neck, who was wandering past with a rather stupid expression on his face. Satisfied that he was unobserved, Brander took the lift to the fifth floor.

The doors to the flats all looked alike. He stopped at one and peered down at the name plate. His heart was beating wildly and his leg still throbbed. He pressed the bell.

The blonde girl who opened the door had obviously been crying very recently. He thought he recognized her.

"Oh, it's you again, is it. Well you can't come in just now," she said at once.

"Who's there?" A voice came from inside the flat.

"It's me—Brander. I have to speak to you."

Whitehall, Tuesday Teatime

The desk was covered with crumpled-up paper. It was a tedious process. He had the letter or rather the page of figures, and he had the cypher book, but that was only the beginning. He had to find where they fitted in with one another, and this was taking time. Perhaps Brander hadn't even worked from that book. It could have been from the one that presumably had been in the other sealed envelope.

Page by page, he worked through it. Brander had marked some numbers with a pencilled line, which could indicate where one message began and the other stopped. But here too there was no quick way of discovery. Time and time again, the numbers and the first figures in the letter would begin to spell out a word, but then lapse into gibberish.

Time was needed. He must get that message to Jo. Now that she was there, she must realize the impossibility of doing much, of finding out more. He had the clue in his hands, and he needed time to work out what it amounted to. She had to play for time, give the other side the impression that she would lead them to more contacts, more agents. That was the most she could do. If she started to show that she was giving out or coming home, they would pounce. He must tell her that. It was a message to her that she couldn't escape. She had to wait, and the eventual consequences would probably be the same. Armstrong realized that more than she would. He would be asking her to do a great deal.

As he looked at his watch, he noticed his hand was shaking. Tesco should be reporting in soon. He didn't imagine that setting him to tail Brander would lead to anything, but it was worth a try. And Tesco was no trained tail. If only he could have mobilized the organization. They would produce the goods, if there were any. But that was out. Such a request wouldn't be secret long in the organization.

Similarly, he couldn't ask the cyphers section to break the code he was working on. With their computers, they could have told him in ten minutes whether he was barking up the wrong tree. He had to do it himself.

He turned back to the code book. He had got to page seven of the photostat. At this rate it would take days, and he had promised himself that he would be in Berlin by the following evening. He could of course take the stuff with him, and work at it as he went. But that was too risky, and he might arrive at the other end with empty hands.

He had almost given up when he saw the faint trace of a pencilled circle round a number at the top of page thirteen. The mark didn't show up well on the photostat and he nearly missed it. How he wished he had the original.

The letter was tried once again. Again it didn't lead anywhere. The first two groups didn't mean anything. Then he got it. The first groups were merely reference numbers. They might have thrown him off in any case, if it hadn't been for that pencilled circle. He was away at last.

The desk phone beside him began to ring, but he ignored it. He became immersed in his task. In ten minutes he had the first sentence, it was a slow process without someone to read out the numbers for him.

It was in substance a report of recent developments in the organization. It told, in brief English, of the Director's resignation, the Minister's insistence on calling off Sonntag, of the collapse of morale. . . . It mentioned Jo, the reason for the helicopter's dramatic appearance at the Curtain by Helmstedt, the agents—the lot. It was splendid stuff for the other side. A spy . . . the spy would be proud.

There were references throughout to reports from someone referred to as "B"—presumably Brander. He had added one or two pieces about security for good measure, but he was obviously not the author of the message itself. There was no indication of where it had originated. Presumably it wasn't necessary. The recipients knew who was sending the stuff.

So he had been right. The other side knew everything. Everything up until this moment, Armstrong thought grimly. They were waiting to pounce on the lot—five good agents . . . and Jo.

What to do? The Director was the first idea that flashed through his mind. But it would take time to contact him in his garden in Kent, or wherever he was. And then what could he do? He was out of the chair now—away from it all. No. If anything, it had to be a direct approach to the man who had helped increase the mess.

He picked up the telephone.

"Get me the Minister's Private Secretary, please."

"There's someone who has been urgently trying to get you, Mr Armstrong," the operator responded. "A Mr Tesco. He sounds foreign. He's going to ring back in ten minutes. I told him that I thought you must be out."

"I will be, I'm afraid. I have to go out again. Tell him to leave a number where he can be contacted."

"Yes, Sir. Putting you through now to the Private Secretary."

"Hello? This is Armstrong here. I want to see the Minister urgently . . . What? . . . Instructions not to arrange appointments with *any* of us? How the . . . How does he expect to do his bloody job then? . . . Sorry! I didn't quite mean that. But I must see him . . . You can't? . . . But I insist. O.K., O.K., I know you have to obey orders. In the circumstances, I invoke codeword 'Mayflower'."

Armstrong hesitated before using the word which meant "extreme emergency". He would have to justify it later. It worked, though, and the Private Secretary's tone changed to a more respectful key.

"I'll be round straight away. Yes, I'll wait till the Minister is free, so long as it's not more than half an hour. There is no time to lose."

As he went out, Armstrong passed the glass-fronted

telephone exchange. The operator looked at him oddly as he disappeared down the stairs. She had obviously been listening in to the call. She dialled the lads in the registry and told them there was a crisis brewing. Nothing like a bit of gossip to brighten the day.

FIFTEEN

Westminster, Tuesday Evening

"I had nourished the happy thought that I had seen the last of you. You had better have a good story this time. And as for using 'Mayflower'. Don't you know when it's used, we have to make up a new codeword?"

It wasn't a happy beginning, but Armstrong hadn't expected it to be. He spoke formally.

"I have here proof of the involvement of a senior member of the organization in passing secret information to the other side."

"So?—I always assumed that half you lot would be working for someone else. The existence of the organization outside the field of normal democratic controls just asks for this sort of thing. But if someone is a traitor, then it's a matter for Special Branch, not for me. Let me have a written report. Now I have work to do. Would you mind leaving . . ."

"I'm afraid I'm not finished, Minister." Armstrong allowed a hard note to creep into his voice, and it caused the Minister to look up in astonishment. Before he could say anything, Armstrong went on: "And I came to see you personally, because, Minister, whether you like it or not, you are very much involved in this whole affair. I think you would like to hear about it now, for your own—er—good."

"Are you trying to . . . ?"

"No, Minister, I am not trying to threaten you. You accused me of trying to do that once before. All I'm trying to do is to salvage a little from the wreckage which we— you as well, if you don't mind me saying so—have created. And this time, Minister, there is no lack of human warmth in me. What I am trying to get you to allow me to do is . . . to save a few lives—lives of people I care about, not just names in a report."

"What sort of game are you trying to play?"

"I can see I will have to spell it out, then." Armstrong was the angry one now, angry at the self-righteous attitude of the Minister. He realized he had to get the upper hand without provoking too much of a reaction from the man—that might make him refuse to listen to anything.

"I have a report here which was intercepted by our people in Berlin. I've managed, by a peculiar coincidence, to decode it, and it shows that someone highly placed in the organization has been telling the other side everything about our work—not just the Sonntag thing." He paused briefly.

"Go on, go on, if you must."

"This report, presumably one of a series, as the reference number is fairly high, for example reports in full the collapse of morale and the disintegration of the upper levels of the organization, following the attitude adopted towards it by the Minister responsible for . . ."

"I don't believe it," the Minister said, but his remark didn't carry conviction.

Armstrong went on in slow, measured terms, doing his best to rub the message home as hard as he could:

". . . responsible for its efficient working. It suggests that your pacifist attitudes, and here I quote directly from the report, mean that the organization and all its work in the field will become completely ineffectual, so long as you are in charge. It goes on to suggest how the resultant defencelessness can be exploited. . . ."

"Shut up a minute, Armstrong. Let me think."

Armstrong sat silently, congratulating himself on winning at least the first round. But there was still a long way to go.

"Do you know who is responsible?"

"Well, one of them, I think, is a man called Brander. He is Head of Security. You'll realize how serious that is in itself."

"And there are others?"

"I think there must be. He was referred to in the report, but it doesn't seem to have originated from him."

"What have you done about it so far? Who has been informed, and what action are they taking?"

"I have done nothing except come to see you, Minister. The report is correct. There is no one to go to in the organization. As you know, the Director did away with a deputy, and worked directly to his heads of department. The only man, in other circumstances I could have gone to see would have been . . . Brander himself."

"I see. Yes. I'm beginning to understand you, Armstrong. I'm beginning, God help me, to think you did the right thing. Now, what the hell to do now. I must tell the P.M., for a start."

"Not yet, if I might suggest. There is still time to try and save something from it all—no matter what the future of the organization is. By save, I mean save people. There are five or six agents, people who are loyal to us, who are about to be arrested. You know as well as I do that they won't even come to trial. Five men and the girl you heard about."

"What? Is she there. Did you disobey . . . ?"

"No, Minister," Armstrong said wearily. "She more or less escaped, and went over herself. She really did want to find out who murdered her fiancé. The other side know about the lot of them, and are waiting to pounce. They just want to be sure they've got everyone first."

"So where do we go from here? I agree that lives are the most important factor."

To give him his due, Armstrong thought, the Minister was more interested in the agents now than in his own position. It had taken the threat of attacking the Minister's loyalty—something in the way of proof that his pacifism might do the nation great harm—to focus his mind on the issue. But now he wasn't concerned with his own position.

"I thought I might go across."

"And what bloody good would that do? You'd get picked up, too. I saw the report how nearly you *were*, even this side of the Curtain."

"Yes. That's right. I would be. But then I would talk to them . . ."

"You'd do what?"

"I'd suggest a swap to them."

"Swap."

"In the past, Minister, we have swapped spies. We

have a couple of their men in Brixton Prison at the moment. You know the two. They've done eighteen months of the twenty years they were given at the Old Bailey. It's worth a try. We know they would like them back. It's good for the morale of spies on both sides when they know their governments are prepared to arrange exchanges. Good for recruitment, too."

"If I agree, then what? I'll have to get the Cabinet's blessing too, and none of my colleagues like this exchange business in any case. But suppose it works. We'll be back to square one."

"More or less, Minister, except that we'll have laid the traitor."

"But five men and a girl, for two. Not a fair swap to me."

"Our six are minor by comparison. It should work."

"Aren't you forgetting yourself? You'll be there, too. You're a good catch!"

"Thank you for the compliment, Minister, but that's nothing to worry about. I'm only the messenger-boy. They'll let me back. . . ."

"I don't believe you, Armstrong, and I can't agree to it. If there is a crisis this big on hand, I need you here."

"But, Sir . . ."

A telephone rang on the Minister's desk. He picked it up. "It's for you," he said.

"I'll take it outside."

"No, no. Stay here."

Armstrong took the receiver.

"Hello."

"It's me, Tesco. I've been trying to get you for hours."

"I can't speak now, I'm with the Minister."

"O.K. Have it your own way. Perhaps you'll listen when it comes to the funeral."

"What are you talking about?"

"Brander, of course. He's dead. Broken neck. Fell down a lift shaft—from the fifth floor. Lift gate seems to have been opened. I got all the details. First journalist on the spot. Even some photographs. You want them?"

"Brander dead?" Armstrong looked at the Minister as he spoke. The Minister stared back in silence.

"Hello, Tesco. Are you still there? . . . Good. Now what was it? Accident, suicide?"

"The police have ruled out an accident. Apparently there was one with this lift a year or so ago and there were special safety gates fitted then. No, they say some-one must have forced the gates open."

"Then suicide?"

"If you were going to commit suicide, would you jump down a lift shaft? I personally would get claustrophobia before I got to the bottom. Answer: no. You'd jump off a roof like everyone else. . . ."

"O.K., so?"

"Well, I don't want to go into the details on this line, but my guess is . . . well, a woman friend of yours whom he went to meet, is missing. I went to call on her—in my journalist capacity of course—and all I found was a hysterical girl friend of hers—by the name of Liz. Yes, Miss Frances Dixon has taken her passport and left town. Pretty quick too . . ."

"Look, meet me in half an hour, at the flat. I can't keep the Minister waiting any longer. . . ." Armstrong hung up.

"I apologize, Minister, for using your phone," Armstrong remarked stupidly.

"Perhaps it's as well you did. I heard. Who was that on the line?"

"A man called Tesco—a German gossip columnist. We had to arrest him recently for knowing too much about the case. . . ."

"Then he's not reliable?"

"More so than most, Minister. He won't spill anything. He's too frightened. But we can trust him. In fact I was considering sending him over with a message to Jo . . . to Miss Weinberg. She's got to play along and give us time to . . ."

"Yes, that reminds me. What now?"

"Well, I was going to go over. . . ."

"No, you were not. I have a longer memory than that. You'll have to find someone else. If there are murderers around too, then it's all the more important that you stay."

"Minister, did you hear that other name—of the woman that disappeared. She's in Personnel. I imagine she's out of the country by now. We can't even try to stop her, in the circumstances. But I have an idea. Before he—er—left, the Director gave me an indication that he suspected something about her. . . ."

"Are you suggesting I get the Director back?"

"I leave that to you."

"Would he come?"

"I think so, if you asked him."

"I see." The Minister sat down, visibly shaken. "I think you've got me, Armstrong. You're clever, you lot are. But tell me why really you want to go across yourself? Why don't you get someone to take the message about the proposed exchange for you? Why don't we use normal diplomatic channels? I can see we want it handled very carefully, but . . .'

Armstrong realized he had half won the battle. It wasn't entirely necessary, but for some reason he told the Minister about Jo. It was his fault that she was where she was.

The Minister looked at him curiously. "Do you know, Armstrong, I think you're human too—after all."

Whitehall, Tuesday Evening

The clerk hesitated at the door-way.

"Mr Brander said to give you this, this evening. But I suppose it's O.K. if I pass it on to you now, in the circumstances." He handed Armstrong the envelope.

Armstrong opened it quickly, and glanced at the note. Had Brander been on the side of the angels all the time, or was this just an insurance policy? He gave him the benefit of the doubt.

SIXTEEN

West Berlin, Thursday Afternoon

They said it was the coldest winter they could remember since nineteen forty-eight, and that had been a particularly bitter year, emphasized by the scarcity of fuel in the ruined city. The trees that had remained in the Tiergarten after the bombing had been torn down secretly at night to provide warmth.

The street in Charlottenburg still showed much of what those post-war years had been like. It was dowdy, with numerous bomb sites, and the houses that remained showed the scars of war and defeat. Many of them, particularly at that end of the street which spilled into the half-forgotten canal, seemed ready to topple down. The house in which they were waiting had the pock-marks of bullets still round each window, where, perhaps, Russian soldiers had tried to pick off some last defender of the Third Reich.

They waited in silence behind the dirty net curtains. The room was empty except for two packing cases and a pile of rotting newspapers in the corner. The German policeman smoked a small cigar, the others stood or leaned on the peeling walls, waiting, and trying to keep warm. It had been a long wait for some of them. If they had all arrived at once, it would have attracted attention. Armstrong and the young Lieutenant had been the last to come.

"Remember, no action until I say so." Armstrong addressed Head of the Berlin Station. "If we pick them up straight away, we'll only get the little boys, and it may put our people on the other side at risk. I want to get the top man himself."

"I can't see why they should want the army car in the first place. We all know it's easy to get over. The Wall, unlike the Curtain, is full of holes."

"The Curtain is pretty tattered in places too. But nonetheless my guess is that it's the little chap himself who wants to get out. Hennik's description fits the one given by the lorry driver, and Miss Dixon obviously had time to pass the message that we're looking out for him. After nearly being picked up in the restaurant last week, he'll feel doubly cautious. He'll know you have checks on all the exits, but'll realize you'd never control all the army cars that go over. They're doing routine runs through the Wall all the time and in normal circumstances it might have worked."

"O.K. You're probably right. We've got all the cars ready to follow in case," Head of Berlin Station grudgingly agreed.

"When we've run him to earth, I'm going in after him myself."

"But he'll be armed and we'll need all our resources if we've to make sure."

"That's an order. I want to talk to him."

"Talk to him?"

At that moment the Lieutenant broke in: "The corporal's going in now, Sir. He was very nervous when I briefed him. I hope . . ."

"He'd be nervous in this situation in any case, Lieutenant. That's the least of our worries. He's right on time, though," Armstrong said. They all looked at their watches. It was exactly four o'clock.

Head of Berlin Station tried to question Armstrong further but got no response. He shrugged and then took the small cigar the policeman offered him. If Armstrong wanted to kill himself, that was his own affair, but Berlin was still his responsibility.

They waited a further quarter of an hour. The Lieutenant said: "I don't suppose there's a back way out, is there?"

"Even if there is, we've got the car under observation," Armstrong replied.

"Yes, of course. Silly of me." Once again there was silence. The Lieutenant kept watch at the window.

"Here's Corporal Hennik again, Sir. What's . . . ? No, wait a minute, it's someone else in corporal's uniform. Don't recognize him. He's not little, though."

"Anyone with him?"

"No, Sir. He's going towards the car now."

"O.K. Let's go, Lieutenant. The others can deal with the house inmates. Make sure they don't get any messages out." Armstrong went towards the door.

Head of Berlin Station was annoyed. Who the hell did Armstrong think he was? Make sure they don't get any messages out—indeed! He knew his job.

Outside, the two men hurried as fast as they could on the powdery snow. They saw the green Humber pull out from the parking-place and drive off along the street.

Armstrong and the Lieutenant got into the big Mercedes which already had its engine running. Their driver, a German policeman, pulled away before they had the doors shut. Turning round in the back seat, Armstrong could see the rest going into the house.

Fortunately, the new driver of the Humber was obviously not too used to the British car, and the Mercedes caught up with it easily.

Lucky there's only one of them so far, Armstrong thought. He's less likely to spot us.

The car drove up Kantstrasse, and then turned left towards the Tiergarten. Despite the snow, the traffic was fairly heavy, and they nearly lost it once or twice. When it hit Ernst Reuter Platz, it turned right up towards the Brandenburg Gate and the Wall. Just round the corner, it almost stopped, and the driver of the Mercedes had to overshoot it, so as not to appear too obvious. This manœuvre almost made them miss seeing the little man jump into the green car. Armstrong caught a glimpse of someone almost drowned in a khaki peaked cap, and an army greatcoat.

"Pull in, and let them overtake," he ordered. "But don't look at it as it passes."

Out of the corner of his eye he saw the other car shoot past, a small figure in army uniform huddled in the back.

"Alert all cars to cover the exits through the Wall— especially Checkpoint Charlie. It's bound to be there."

The driver passed on the order over the car wireless.

"Now say you're going off the air for security purposes." Again the driver passed on the instruction.

Armstrong could have kicked himself almost immediately thereafter. The army car, instead of turning down towards the Checkpoint, as expected, swung round in a U-turn in the middle of the wide boulevard, and headed back up towards the centre of the town.

"He's going back," the Lieutenant said.

"Very observant," Armstrong muttered angrily, and the other man sulked into silence.

"Can you get the other cars again?" he asked the driver.

"Not immediately. You told me . . ."

"I know, I know. O.K. Well, we mustn't lose him now."

It is always surprising to the visitor how big West Berlin really is. Somehow, there is an impression that it's like some medieval walled town, tiny and compact. In reality, comparatively large areas of countryside are inside its artificial confines.

Towards one of these, the army car headed. The Mercedes had to drive hard to keep up. It had been easy in the built-up areas, but when they reached the suburbs and then the Grünewald, Armstrong realized that the fact they were following, must stick out like a sore thumb.

After about twenty minutes, it became obvious that the occupants of the first car knew this to be the case. They made several attempts to shake off the Mercedes, but the police driver knew both his car and his way about Berlin. Eventually, perhaps realizing that it was impossible to get rid of the tail, they appeared to stop trying. They drove south-west towards the bottom of the great Berlin lake—the Havel.

The Mercedes generally kept the other car well in view, but when they were nearly at the water's edge, the green car suddenly pulled into a side track among the trees, and for a few moments it was hidden from view. By the time they had caught up with it, it was stationary and empty, its doors open and its engine still running. The police driver skidded the Mercedes to a broadside halt on the snow, and Armstrong and the Lieutenant jumped out.

What remains of the once great Berlin Forest is now well laid out with paths and beds of flowers. Even under the snow, one could see that all was tidy and ordered. The park benches and the little rustic signs which pointed the ways to a hundred beauty spots looked forlorn, but the neatness was indisputable.

Neatness that was, except for the two rows of footsteps running away from the parked car.

"Stay here," Armstrong shouted to the driver. "You come with me, Lieutenant. But no shooting, understand?" He noticed that the officer had a revolver in his hand. The other man nodded, and they set off at a run, following the footprints.

The going was slow. The snow, though not deep, had drifted, and they kept stumbling and falling. The tracks ran through among the trees, and the two men could not see more than a few yards ahead. Apart from that, it was now almost dark, and the bushes, black against the white ground, added to the confusion.

Suddenly, they were by the water's edge. The lake was frozen solid, but the trees had stopped, and the ground levelled out into the distance. On the far side, the lights were beginning to come on.

Out across the lake, they could see the two other men. They were running down to the south of a little island which nearly touched the mainland at one point. In summer, it was known for its birds; its name was Peacock Island. They could make out the silhouette of the small castle on it.

"They are going towards the wire," the officer shouted to Armstrong.

"What wire?"

"The border with the Zone runs across the middle of the lake there. There's no wall of course, but there are underwater nets and wire, and it's heavily guarded."

They continued running. Ahead, the floodlights had come on, marking where free Berlin ended.

Armstrong hoped that the other two might be less fit, and the little man, he could see, looked as if he were flagging. He still had on the heavy army greatcoat.

Armstrong knew he wouldn't make it. He saw they were nearly at the boundary, and there were searchlights from the other side playing across the ice as if looking for something.

Armstrong stopped, the officer beside him. He cupped his hands and shouted to the other two to stop. They carried on, though, and in despair, Armstrong followed.

He had left the Lieutenant a little behind, when suddenly he saw the frozen line of buoys, and the wire less than a hundred yards ahead. The two men he was pursuing stopped just short of it, and waited. Armstrong could see why. A party of men were advancing across the ice on the other side. They stopped opposite the fugitives and threw something over. It seemed to be a roll of something—of wooden slats tied together.

The man in corporal's uniform, ran over it easily, to join the group, and the little man began to follow.

"Stop, I want to talk to you, urgently. Stop!"

The little man continued on his way, but then hesitated at the top of the ramp. He stood there, swaying in the darkness, and then turned round and looked down at Armstrong.

"Who are you?" he shouted back in English.

"Sonntag, I want to talk to you."

"What about Sonntag?"

"We both know what I mean." Armstrong wished he could make out the other man's face.

"Then talk." The little man swayed, and nearly fell. The men on the other side were shouting something at him, presumably telling him to come over.

"We can't here, in the middle of the ice."

"All right. Come on over." The little man was mocking him.

"I have a proposition for you."

"Go on."

At that moment, someone behind Armstrong fired, and the little man jumped down from the ramp to the other side. The group on the other side started shooting too, and Armstrong threw himself flat on the ice, cursing the Lieutenant. There was a bang close beside him and he remembered nothing more, except vague lights and noise.

He came to in the back of an ambulance. The Lieutenant was bending over him.

"Are you all right?"

"You bloody fool," Armstrong muttered in reply.

"It wasn't me. The others turned up. They started the shooting, I'm afraid. Head of Berlin Station said he thought he got the little man."

Armstrong put his hand up to his head, and felt it was wet and sticky.

"You weren't hit directly, the doctor says. Probably a chip of ice got you on the temple. Instant anaesthetic. It'll hurt later."

SEVENTEEN

East Berlin, Thursday Evening

The little man sat back uncomfortably in the corner seat of the compartment. The escort placed himself opposite Miss Dixon. A notice had been stuck on the door leading to the corridor indicating that the compartment had been specially reserved by *Intourist*.

The train pulled slowly out of the station. The dull gas lights on the platform, moving past the window, reminded him of London in wartime. This was the impression that East Berlin always left with him; shabbiness and the need for paints other than brown and dark green on the houses.

The train gathered speed. The escort stood up and pulled down the blinds, shutting out the cold night. He closed the ones on the other side as well, to avoid the curious stares of the passengers standing in the crowded corridor.

Why couldn't they have sent a car? Wasn't the catch worth it? The exertions of his narrow escape that afternoon surely deserved better treatment. But of course, he had been living too long in the capitalist West. This was luxury treatment, with a compartment to themselves. He squared his shoulders resignedly against the hard plastic back of the seat.

"Three hours' journey to Leipzig," he explained

helpfully. Miss Dixon thanked him, and then closed her eyes. She was obviously just pretending to sleep. She didn't want to talk to him and the feeling was mutual. He glanced across at the escort, a stupid man with a slightly Mongolian face, who hadn't even taken off his green leather coat, despite the heat in the compartment. Obviously he hadn't heard of deodorant, or perhaps it was too much of a decadent luxury.

He looked back at Miss Dixon. Perhaps she really was asleep now. Her mouth hung unpleasantly open. He realized that she would be under no illusion about the hazards of what she was doing, that she was no longer in a permissive society, no longer her own master. It was the price she had to pay for things going wrong.

But he estimated that someone like her certainly would have no wish to spend the rest of her life as a defector, especially one wanted for murder. She would know too well what it would be like. She had been useful, so she would get one of those dowdy flats in the suburbs, and a meagre stipend every month, perhaps, if she was lucky, working as a translator for one of the propaganda agencies. No, she wasn't the type to remain contentedly in exile. They would have to watch her.

And then there was the murder. That Brander had asked for it, there was no doubt. There would have been other ways. But Miss Dixon had panicked. Now she said she had felt no qualms—rather the reverse: a certain satisfaction that he was out of the way.

The little man closed his eyes and tried to recreate the workings of her mind. He enjoyed such intellectual exercises. The hard decision for her would have been leaving London. But she would see no other immediate alternative. If she had stayed, she would have been arrested. Now she could disappear for a bit, and then later, when she was ready, she would try to go back, taking with her some justification for her action. It would be easy to think of something, and difficult to prove the contrary. The little man, if he had been in Miss Dixon's shoes, would have opted for blaming Brander for the whole thing, perhaps suggesting that he had arranged her abduction as part of a wider conspiracy. . . .

He opened his eyes. The escort was asleep too. There was no danger that she would run away yet, otherwise she wouldn't have come over. For the moment an escort was a mere courtesy.

He wondered what they had in store for her. A debriefing first of all. And she would give them it. She had everything to gain. She would drag it out and keep appearing to be useful. That way she would expect to live a better life and would be well placed to go back.

He reviewed his first assumption that she would want to go back. He remembered the confidential report on her had emphasized that self-preservation had always been her driving force, that, and the pursuit of her own pleasures. It wasn't on political grounds that they had managed to recruit her. If anything, she was anti-communist: its credo hardly agreed with what she wanted out of life. No, her driving force had been the dislike of the society she perpetually found herself in, that of a male-dominated one.

The destruction of this environment had been Miss Dixon's motivation ever since she had been a student. Her tutor had called her a "natural anti-", and she hadn't denied it. It had been an easy extension for them to recruit her. They had suggested they had a little more respect for the non-male.

The train pulled into another gas-lit station. The little man pulled aside the blind and looked out. Perhaps it was only the weather and the hour of the night, but the waiting passengers seemed so cold and lifeless. The escort woke up, looked curiously at Miss Dixon and then across at him.

"Coffee?" he asked. The little man nodded, and Miss Dixon opened her eyes. In a few moments, a white-jacketed waiter appeared with a tray, cups, biscuits and coffee—better coffee than on many West European railways, he thought to himself.

He looked at his watch. Another hour or so still. He closed his eyes again and slept.

The little man was first on the platform when the train came in. It was a few minutes late. There had been some snow on the line. He pulled up the collar of his coat against the cold. A railway porter wheeled past a trolley, piled high with mail bags and almost knocked him over. It added to his bad temper.

The woman with the escort came up behind him.

"What now," she asked with a smile. He gave an involuntary shudder.

"We have arranged a room for you for the night at the Central Hotel. It's very comfortable I'm told. It's for foreign visitors, mainly," he said, as if this explained why it should be comfortable. "There should be a car outside."

Leipzig, Thursday Night

Tesco was feeling pleased with himself. He had delivered Armstrong's message personally to the girl, and he was sure he hadn't been seen doing so. She had almost greeted him when she saw him in the bar, but the look in his eyes warned her off, and after a slight start, she turned away from him and ordered a drink.

He had sat with a Western colleague, drinking atrocious East German whisky and talking about nothing in particular. He had watched her out of the corner of his eye, marvelling at her composure. He looked round, searching for a way of getting the message across.

When she finished her drink, she made to leave, and he had simultaneously excused himself, and followed her into the reception hall. Then, quite deliberately, he had gone up behind her and tripped her up. She almost fell.

"Sprain your ankle," he whispered amid loud apologies. He helped her over to a couch, overwhelming her with protestations of regret. He called for a waiter in a loud voice, demanding cold water, a towel, and a brandy. He then settled down beside her, and continued his solicitations for the benefit of any onlookers. As he did so, he managed to pass on the message, and answer one or two questions she put to him.

"Armstrong's coming over," he whispered. "I'm not quite sure what for. He's got some scheme . . .

"I am *so* sorry, Madame, for having caused you . . ."
He broke off as a waiter approached.

Eventually he said: "It's not safe enough here. I'll contact you later." Then he stood up, bowed as far as the circularity of his figure would let him, and once more apologizing, returned to his drink at the bar.

Yes, Tesco was pleased with himself. A good job well done. He ordered another whisky, this time with lemonade to drown the taste. It nearly choked him, for at that instant, he saw Miss Dixon come into the room.

EIGHTEEN

Leipzig, Friday Night

Reaching above his head, he pulled himself over the railings on to the balcony. Above, the rusty fire-escape stretched into the darkness. The metal steps were cold and wet and he had to climb carefully to avoid slipping.

He counted the windows as he passed them. At the fifth he stopped, and leaning over, he pushed gently at the pane. It gave a fraction. Thank God. A knock might have attracted attention. To have been pulled in as a cat burglar would have been too futile.

He stepped over the sill, gripping with his fingers on the damp stone wall. He pushed, and the window swung open against the curtain. Gently he eased himself into the room. Tesco had better have been right about the number.

Steadying himself on the floor, he turned to close the window, since the wind was blowing the curtains across the room. He knocked against a chair and it scraped slightly against the woodwork.

"Who's there?" a startled voice said in German. He froze against the wall.

"Who's there?" the voice repeated. With relief he recognized her despite the unfamiliar language.

"Not so loud. It's the milkman."

"Paul! How . . . ?"

"Hush. Stay where you are. Don't put on the light. I can just see my way."

"Am I glad to see you! But how . . . ?"

"Shhh. . . ."

"What are you doing?"

"It's a bit cold. You don't mind me getting in beside you, do you. I can't find a chair."

"Paul, do be serious."

"But I am, very. Sheets and blankets deaden noise, reduce risk of eavesdropping." He lay back on the pillow beside her.

"I got your message from Tesco," she whispered, adopting his caution, "but I didn't expect you so soon." She felt reassured by the warmth of his body, but still trembled at the aftermath of the fright he had given her.

"We haven't much time. I have something to arrange . . ."

"But isn't it dangerous for you here? Why did you come?"

"I've a bit of exchange and mart to do. I couldn't find anyone else." She looked at him oddly, raising herself up on the pillow and trying, by the thin light in the room, to make out the expression on his face.

He moved yet closer beside her and told her the plan. They'd be bound to agree. . . . She had helped greatly. . . . Now that they knew most of what had happened to Alex and who the traitor was, it only remained to get everyone home and dry.

She nearly believed him. But like the Minister, she was dubious about his arithmetic. Two men in Brixton into six men and a girl in Leipzig don't go. She remembered the Gerald Brooke affair.

He didn't try too hard to persuade her. The proximity

helped. He rolled over beside her and stifled her whispered protests with his mouth.

For an hour or so they relaxed in the best of all good ways. The tensions of the preceding days sweated out of them, and then they lay side by side, naked under the single sheet. They slept a little.

"Good evening, Mr Armstrong, good evening, Miss Weinberg." The electric light blinded their eyes. In natural reaction, they both clutched the sheet against themselves as they sat up in bed and faced Miss Dixon.

"Tut, and it's not even a double room, Mr Armstrong," she mocked. "Very immoral, trying to get a free bed for the night. They can't pay you very well if you're reduced to this."

Two men in green leather coats stood behind her, pistols in their hands. They looked unblinkingly unmoved by the proceedings: doubtless they had witnessed such things before. The blankness in their expressions might also have something to do with a lack of knowledge of English. They looked Caucasian, rather than East German.

"Get up!"

"We'd like to get dressed." Armstrong showed the natural hesitance of any man caught *in flagrante*.

"Of course you would. But I'm not shy, neither are my colleagues." She gestured towards the greencoats. They looked at her enquiringly.

"Get up!" she repeated. "And stand over by the wall." They moved slowly, urged on by the sight of the pistols.

"A beautiful figure, if I may say so." She hardly glanced

at the naked man, but moved a step towards Jo. The latter's look brought her back to the matter in hand.

"Ah well. Never mind just now. There's lots of time. Just stand where you are . . . No, don't touch the clothes. I have some questions to ask, and a little fresh air may help you to answer them." She went over to the window and threw it open. The bitter night cold hit them quickly.

"Now turn round!" Neither of them moved.

"Turn round, I said!" She raised her voice, and the green-coats automatically raised their guns with it. They moved slowly round. The cold freshened Armstrong's courage.

"What the hell do you think you're playing at?" His composure returned and he went forward and seized his trousers. He didn't look up as he did so. If he was going to be shot for covering himself, it was in a good cause.

"Leave him, then. But keep the girl where she is." Miss Dixon spoke to the green-coats in German. They went forward and held her upright and facing Miss Dixon.

"What the hell d'you think you're doing?" Armstrong shouted at her. "Tell your men friends to leave the girl alone at once, or . . ."

"Or you'll what, Mr Armstrong. No. Stay where you are or there might be an accident. These two have their orders, and I believe they know their jobs."

"Relax, Paul. Shouting won't help. I'm O.K.," Jo murmured. She was shivering.

"For God's sake, let the girl get dressed."

"I said I have some questions to ask. If we get through them quickly, then I'll put aside my selfish pleasure at this charming sight and let her dress."

"What d'you want?"

"Can't you guess. I've been listening in a bit—they have the room wired, of course. They told me you were here. Unfortunately I came in during the love-play which was certainly amusing and I heard quite a lot, but . . ."

She would have missed the early part, the plans of the swap and so forth, Armstrong thought rapidly. They had talked under the bed-clothes till then. It was only later and relaxed, that they had been less cautious. She would want to know why he was here, and how much he had on her, though the latter must be of academic interest, since her behaviour over the past few minutes. Unless of course she thought only he knew, and perhaps the girl . . . After all, who could he be working with in London? The organization was in ruins. . . .

"That must have been a disappointment. . . ."

"All right, Armstrong. Enough is enough. I'm asking you first why you are here. You're not following me by any chance?"

"Me, following Miss Dixon. Why should I do that? I'm not your type, am I? No, I came over looking for a spy and a murderer. . . ."

"So Brander did tell you?" She stiffened.

"That you shoved him down the lift? No, he couldn't do that, poor man. About the spying though . . . what's your guess?" He was pretty sure she was working as much in the dark as he was. She had gone over and wanted to know how much she was missed. He'd keep her guessing if he could.

When she spoke again, her voice was sharper. "You

weren't after me. The organization or what's left of it, doesn't work that way. I should know. You're on your own here, or looking for her. You're backing up a hunch. You had an interest in knowing where I'd gone, of course, and what I'd done. Perhaps you thought of stopping me debriefing myself fully when I got here. But no. You'd realize there would be little chance of that once I was away. The people here aren't so careless. . . ." Miss Dixon suddenly realized she was rambling on, like a hysterical woman. She stopped short. "All right. Once again, what are you after?"

"I thought a nice holiday in the sun . . ."

"That will do, Armstrong. I've had enough. I want to know why you are here, and who . . . whether anyone put you up to it?"

"Head of Security asked me as a favour." Armstrong forced himself to continue to banter, to reassure himself and give Jo encouragement, and also because he saw it was very much irritating Miss Dixon. He wasn't sure what he'd gain by provoking her, but it might help to clarify matters.

Slowly now, slowly. Think carefully. She obviously wanted to know whether he was on his own. Why not tell her what she wanted to hear? Let her think it was a stupid heroic gesture to save the girl . . . well, it was partly true. Miss Dixon was only a by-product of the trip. But if she thought he alone knew all about it back in London, then she might return. He could see that she wouldn't want to spend the rest of her days as a fugitive. And if the other side, while he was bargaining with them, were to learn that she wasn't entirely loyal to them too, they might be annoyed, despite her earlier service. There were a lot of "ifs".

"Let the girl put some clothes on," Armstrong said. "She's freezing."

"She wasn't wearing much else when we came in. She presumably wasn't freezing then." Miss Dixon laughed. "Last time. What are you up to?"

"Winter sports." He tried to throw a reassuring glance at Jo, but Miss Dixon intervened.

"Just to remind you where we are, Armstrong. Put the girl over the bed." She barked the last words out in German to the two green-coats. They moved forward.

Armstrong lunged forward, but one of the men stopped him with his gun.

"Over the bed," she repeated in German. The men grabbed Jo and threw her violently down on her face. As she fell, she succeeded in dealing one of the green-coats a kick which sent him retching in pain. Armstrong again moved forward, but this time Miss Dixon had the gun, and again he stopped short. The other green-coat was easily holding Jo face downwards on the mattress.

"I'll leave you in no doubt what I'm going to do, Mr Armstrong." Miss Dixon went across to the open window and took from a hook on the wall, a heavy plaited sash which was used during the day for tying the curtains back.

"I've done this before, but I usually don't get such pleasure free. The way to spoil my enjoyment is to answer my questions." She raised the sash.

"O.K., O.K. Put it down. I'll talk. It's like this. The organization has crumbled. There was no one left. Besides, there wasn't time, or I might have . . . I wasn't after you. How was I to know where you had come . . . ?"

"For God's sake, Paul, stop!" Jo called a muffled shout from the bed. The green-coat pulled her arms sharply behind her, and she gave a short cry.

"Sorry, Jo, I can't let . . ." He would make her believe he was cracking. She might not be able to act it out anyway.

"No," she managed to cry as Miss Dixon brought the sash heavily down on her naked back.

"That will do, Miss Dixon. You are not in London now."

"You were leaving this to me." She looked round angrily at the little man who now stood in the doorway.

"I am not going to have a public debate with you. All I will say is that I don't approve of your methods. Let the girl go," he ordered. "Get dressed, you two."

"Nice to see you again," Armstrong said.

"One of my colleagues was quite badly injured. I hardly feel that event was a good beginning to your suggested exchange of trust."

A fading photograph of the Chairman of the Central Committee hung on the wall above the desk. Armstrong settled back in the plastic-covered armchair and looked across at the little man. His command of English was almost perfect.

"It was a mistake, and directly counter to my orders. I would hardly have come over here . . ."

"Very well. I accept that. Now what is your proposition. Time is short."

Miss Dixon and the green-coats had disappeared,

and Jo, despite his protestations, had also gone. He was alone with the little man, yet he felt more relaxed than he had done for some time. He almost began to feel that this was someone with whom he could work. He could see that there was almost a measure of warmth in the other man's attitude, despite the unfavourable circumstances. Rather like politics where members of two different parties can be closer to each other in outlook than with colleagues in the same party, so could the intelligence community often have more in common and in sympathy with the spies on the other side than with laymen on their own.

The little man took a nail-file from his pocket and began polishing his already immaculate fingernails.

"Do begin."

"We believe that you know or are aware of the existence of a very small number of men, of our agents, working over here. . . ."

The little man laid the nail-file down on the desk in front of him and stared across at Armstrong. "If you call five men small. In terms of spying, I would classify it as large, yes, quite large."

Armstrong ignored the remark, and went on: "And you are aware, doubtless, that Her Majesty's Government have, in Brixton prison, two convicted agents . . . from your . . ."

"I see."

"I have been authorized to come and negotiate an exchange."

"Miss Dixon seems to have slipped up. I understood that . . ."

"How unreliable of her. I would watch . . ."

"Be that as it may, Mr Armstrong; but this is most unusual, you would agree." The little man was so precise, Armstrong thought. He must have studied for a long time in Britain.

"You would agree, Mr Armstrong, that when such delicate affairs have been negotiated in the past, it has been done through diplomatic channels."

"The circumstances are slightly different here, Herr . . . You have made no arrests and brought no charges, and no one has been brought to trial."

"Yet."

"Of course, it is up to you. But we felt it might avoid certain difficulties, and possible political repercussions if . . ."

"You mean there might be people in the House of Commons who would think it strange to have British spies in time of peace?"

"We don't want to start hotting up the cold war again. . . ."

"You could have thought of that before."

"Things have changed."

"Of course, of course. What you mean is that spying is all right so long as it doesn't get to be public knowledge that it's going on."

"Some people think that way. Intelligence gathering, but no U.2 type crises. . . . But I have put forward the proposition."

"Five to two is no fair proposition."

"Six. There is the girl. But then we've got four men that we picked up in your house in Charlottenburg."

"Very small fry. You can have them. But you're right. There is the girl as well. I was forgetting. Six to two as you say."

"The six are hardly in the same category. The other two are among the major spies of the postwar period."

"You underestimate your people. Sonntag was well planned. We give you that. If we had not had the fortunate, how shall I put it, service from your headquarters in London, they might have done considerable damage to the defence effort of the Republic."

"Miss Dixon?"

"Precisely."

"Yes . . . of course." Armstrong allowed himself to hesitate a moment too long, and the little man looked curiously across at him. "Yes, Miss Dixon. Nonetheless, the Brixton inmates are potentially valuable to you."

"They have spent their usefulness."

"Come, come. You people like to give long-service-and-good-conduct medals too. Take Miss Dixon for example. Now she will get her rewards . . . won't she? As I said elsewhere recently, it's good for morale and recruitment."

"You'll need a lot of both, from what I understand. But my dear Armstrong, you can't use Miss Dixon as a lever on us. She has little place or importance, I can assure you. A small and rather unpleasant tool in the grand design. Miss Dixon thinks of herself as a queen in this game. She is, however, a pawn discarded at the first move. We don't particularly like murders, especially when they aren't done to order, and the murderer—" The little man shrugged indifferently.

"Surely the information she was providing . . ."

". . . Was useful in its way, certainly it was. But our objective was, and is, a broader and more important one. As to the exchange. Well, the authority is not mine. It may take some time."

"And Miss Weinberg."

"She is under arrest at the moment. Charge is immoral behaviour and false pretences. Her hotel room was only a single. We are strict about that here." The little man laughed. "But don't worry. We'll keep Miss Dixon well away from her."

"You're welcome to her if she wants to . . ."

"If she what . . . ?"

"If, if we knew each other better," Armstrong permitted himself a grin, "then . . . But back to business."

Again the little man looked sharply at Armstrong. He almost began to ask a further question but then he obviously thought better of it. Armstrong was playing some game and they both knew it.

"Two more points. One, your journalist."

"You've got Tesco?"

"Ah, so he is yours."

Armstrong cursed his stupidity.

"Don't worry. He got away. He was clever. He left by plane about an hour ago. He'll be in Paris by now."

"One less to bargain for."

"True. He would have had his uses. He seems to have a good eye for a story."

"And you had a second point?"

"Yes. What to do about you."

"I wondered when you would come to that." They both smiled.

NINETEEN

Near Magdeburg, Monday Night

They lay close together in a shallow ditch by the side of
the autobahn. Less than twenty yards away the heavy
lorries and the cars roared past, headlights brightened
by the snow on the trees. Nine black shapes on the snow,
very obvious to anyone who came close-to. Nine:
Armstrong and the girl, the five agents and two "contact
men".

He knew it must be a trap. It had all been too easy.
Within twenty-four hours they had agreed to everything
he had proposed—almost everything. His own position
hadn't been mentioned again.

They had given him every facility to call London. It
took some time before the call came through and he was
left alone in the bare office. He felt completely cut off,
and it was with a sense of shock when the phone rang
and he got straight through, to the Director himself.

"Welcome back."

"Thank you."

He phrased the message carefully, working in the
agreed words which indicated that he wasn't speaking
under duress. The exact details of the handover would
be delivered by hand via the Berlin Station, within the
hour. There was little else to say. The phone went dead.

He had gone with the little man to pick up the five.

All thought they were being arrested and one of them had been injured by a bullet while trying to get away. Some had already known the game was up and that they were being watched. Partly relieved by Armstrong's assurances, they were mainly old campaigners and silently shared his doubts and his knowledge of the alternative to freedom.

They had been waiting for nearly twenty minutes. It was well below freezing, and none of them was particularly well dressed. The lorry was late. . . .

The arrangements were peculiar enough without the delay. The five were to be hidden in a lorry which was to drive along the autobahn corridor to the border with West Germany at Helmstedt. They would be let through at precisely the same time as the two Brixton internees were handed over at a checkpoint into East Berlin, ninety miles away. Synchronization was to be by wireless. The little man had insisted on the five being hidden. Only the head of the zonal border guards would know they were there. Otherwise, the little man had said, it would all become too public, and as the entire Central Committee hadn't been consulted, there might be trouble. "We have our hard-liners too. Take it or leave it. . . ." Armstrong had taken it. There was no alternative. Spy-swapping wasn't always a popular exercise.

It all sounded a bit thin. Concealment of the five meant that there would be no problem if the guards arrested or shot them "while trying to escape". There was the wireless check. The two were not to be handed over till the five were safe, but . . .

Then there was Jo and himself. She was to go over

later—"our insurance policy," the little man joked. Armstrong asked if he himself was involved. Was he under arrest? He was merely the messenger, remember.

"Yes, just the messenger, of course," was the reply.

Günter Scholz drove very gently in the slow lane. "Three hundred metres after the western turn-off to Magdeburg." Captain Hermes had made him repeat it a dozen times. Surely he was there by now. He thought of the five empty crates buried deep among the ones filled with new refrigerators and washing-machines. The sweat was pouring down his face. He reached forward to turn the heating down in the cab. It was already off, and the cab was cold. He remembered being arrested by the advancing American soldiers in 1944. It had been the same then.

A light flashed quickly five times a little ahead. He drove up to it, switched the engine off, and jumped out. Before doing anything else, he opened the bonnet of the lorry and disconnected an ignition wire as he had been told to do. To suggest a breakdown he left the screw loose, as though it had shaken itself out of the hole.

The men came up to him out of the dark. He wasn't sure how many. He told them which crates were which. They had them out in minutes. They opened easily. One by one the men went in. The others lifted the crates back into the lorry. The nailed boxes were heavy. He was glad there were three others to help. One of them looked familiar.

"O.K. Off you go. Good luck."

He jumped into the cab after reconnecting the ignition

wire. He switched on, and drove slowly off. The whole operation had only taken about ten minutes. Fortunate that no patrols had passed. Hermes had said that was fixed too. He was still sweating, but felt more relaxed now that the first stage was over. Then the engine of the lorry spluttered and cut.

Westminster, Monday Night

"Fine, thank you, Miss Simms. That's all for today, I think. Could you ask Richard to come in with the other files."

Miss Simms picked up her note book and pencils and left thankfully. It had been a hard day, and the Minister hadn't been in the best of tempers. She would type the last bits in the morning, before he came in. Home to bed now.

The Minister swung round in his chair and gazed unseeingly at the bound volumes in the built-in bookcase. The green light from the lamp was relaxing, but he was feeling tired, very tired. Sometime soon he would have to begin thinking of the future. He had no intention of burning himself out in the saddle. He would do what his wife had long been urging him . . . soon.

The Private Secretary hovered in with the files. The Minister wished Richard would appear a little more definite, a little less feminine. Perhaps it was a defence. He never shouted at his Private Secretary.

"Nothing very urgent here, Sir. But I'm afraid the Director is on his way over. He should be here any minute." The Private Secretary looked curiously at the Minister. He had expected a strong reaction. He had always got it in the past, but now the Director was back again everything seemed to be working well. He had heard a rumour that the P.M. had had a hand in it.

"O.K., Richard. In that case you can knock off. I'll wait till he comes. See you in the morning."

"Good night, Minister."

Funny people these Civil Servants. They never showed their feelings. Though Armstrong had—just once. They probably had them underneath just like ordinary mortals. The Minister swung his chair round to the bookcase again.

Take the Director, for example. He had reappeared on the scene just as if he had been on leave. The resignation had hardly been mentioned. They had gone on much as before, with a little more tolerance on his own part, the Minister realized. But still, if *he* had resigned . . .

He wondered what the man was coming about now. Why did he always work at night? He had heard that the Director had worked for Churchill during the war, and perhaps that was the reason. Or it could be the nature of his work?

The Director came in without knocking and immediately sat down without being asked. It was unlike him to be discourteous.

"What is it then, Vincent . . ." The Minister had dropped the title since the return. "You've got a face as long as . . ."

"It's the Sonntag clearing-up operation again. I'm afraid we've got bad news."

"I hate that name. What's gone wrong? Hasn't the handover worked?"

"It's happening about now, Minister, so we don't know for sure yet, but . . ."

"Are they in danger?"

"We've just had a message. We're trying to check. It says in essence that the five will be O.K. so long as we hand over the Brixton people."

"But not Armstrong and the girl?"

"Exactly."

"And so what do we do? Stop the deal?"

"Even if we could in time, I'm not sure that it matters now."

"Yes it does. If we hold up the exchange. We . . . we can make an issue of it, make it public."

"That wouldn't work, Minister. On reflection you'd probably agree. Besides, I've been trying to tell you— the message says they're dead—Armstrong and the girl, that is. There's no confirmation yet and the source is dubious. It's from Miss Dixon."

"Dreadful. Dreadful. Armstrong and the girl. Miss Dixon? You mean . . . ?" The Minister, visibly shaken, stopped in the middle of his sentence.

"Yes, so you see there is every reason to doubt. She has everything to gain by having us believe her. She sent the message for a purpose. She claims to have uncovered the whole affair, the complete counter-plot and says that Brander and Armstrong were in it together."

"You don't believe . . . ?"

"She answers our doubts in advance. She says she has proof. She may . . . anything is possible."

"But it's preposterous to suggest Armstrong may be involved."

L

"Yes. You're right. I've been checking. I blame myself for all this you know. If I had followed my instincts, I would have investigated Brander and Miss Dixon a while back."

"You suspected . . . ?"

"Suspicion is dangerous, and that's why I took only minor action. All I did was to put in train a few minor enquiries—I have the facilities you know. I did a check on where certain highly delicate papers went. Brander and Dixon always got them. They had arranged that themselves, though things like Sonntag were a bit marginal to their interests. We operate a strict "need-to-know-policy" on distribution. In addition I asked myself who knew enough to be able to set a trap for Armstrong up at Helmstedt; and who would know your mind, if you'll excuse me, know it well enough to realize the, er, effect of writing an anonymous letter to you. This narrowed my enquiries down considerably. By the time I left I had found nothing more than that, but I hinted to Armstrong, and he followed it up. Not that I think Brander was in it very deeply. He was a bitter, frustrated man. We would have to have got rid of him anyway. He was bad for morale. He probably got himself hooked by Miss Dixon while trying to pursue one of his vendettas. As far as I can discover he had only been doing the cyphering of messages to Berlin for a few days. His interest in Sonntag before then was probably no more than his practice of keeping his nose in every pie. He didn't have the strength of nerve to be a real traitor, though I detect his style of writing in the letter to you. . . ."

"Yes, the letter. I had forgotten about that. Not that I

apologize for my attitude, you know. I feel most strongly—"

The Director interrupted tactfully: "Miss Dixon says she is trying to get back, as I said."

"Can't wait. I don't believe any of it."

"We'll know when we hear of the exchange."

"So you don't recommend stopping it?"

"In the circumstances . . . and there are five others involved."

"Very well."

"If I may, I'll just confirm your view to the officer on duty. There isn't much time." The Director picked up the phone with the green receiver. He got through immediately. "Carry on," he said briefly.

The two men looked at each other in silence for some minutes. Then the Minister said: "How did this message get to you?"

"It's from the other side all right. It came through a commercial link we used to use. We gave it up as being possibly compromised."

"I see. So you don't think Miss Dixon's honest, but that her message about the killings is?"

"Yes, Minister. I can't see what else to believe."

"Will they let us know straight away?"

"They have instructions to ring through here."

"Then have a drink. You will wait, won't you? They keep Ministers' offices well supplied."

West Berlin, Monday Night
The street leading to Checkpoint Charlie is narrow and

undistinguished. Just before you get to the hut in the middle of the road which houses the Allied Military Police, there are some shops selling souvenirs on one side; a house on the other side has a continuous exhibition in it about the Wall. The shop window is full of photographs of dramatic, of terrifying, of tragic escapes and attempts at escape. Inside, there are charts and more photographs. Up a staircase, and you can see a car on display which, with its special primitive armour plating, had been used in some successful attempt to flee to the West. There is also a closed circuit television camera through which you can watch what is going on on the other side of the Wall, at the Soviet end of the checkpoint. People come and stare at the real life drama of seeing the control and the customs only a few hundred metres away, checking vehicles for smuggled goods or stowaways.

A man stood watching the screen now. It was dark in the exhibition house and the tourists had long gone. The set was still switched on though, and he was watching the lights on the screen intently. He recognized the ones from the cars waiting to come through, the ones from the arc lights of the customs post, and the duller ones from the offices on the other side. Then he saw the flashing light. One-two-three long, one-two-three-four-five short.

The man turned about and felt his way down the steps, across the main room of the exhibition, to the door. As he left, he switched a contact which turned off the TV set for the night.

Outside, one or two late-night tourists, and the curious, looked at him oddly. The German policeman came up and moved them on. The policeman paid no attention to the man, who walked across the road to the van.

A large black van, almost like a Black Maria. There was a radio aerial coming out of the top.

"They're already there."

"Still two minutes," said the person in the driver's seat. The man took out a packet of cigarettes, selected one, and lit it. He knew the other man didn't smoke.

Two minutes passed. The radio in the cab crackled. There was some delay, the voice said. No, they could see the lorry through the binoculars. It was coming to the last barrier—ninety miles away at Helmstedt, where the autobahn ran through the Curtain into the West.

"Carry on," the radio said.

The man who had been watching the television went round to the back of the van. He unlocked the thick steel doors. Two men with guns jumped out. Then two other men, older, obviously hesitant and unsteady on their feet. They both carried small, cheap suitcases.

"Carry on." The man addressed the two travellers. "Straight across. No one will stop you, until you meet your friends."

The two with the suitcases walked towards the Wall. The driver got out of the cab. The men with the guns came round to the front of the vehicle and put their guns away. Everyone, including the German policeman and the Allied soldiers in the hut, watched the two men. They watched curiously. The two men walked faster and faster. They almost broke into a run. They were nearly over.

The radio in the cab was crackling again. It was difficult

to hear what was said. The driver jumped into the cab.

"Cancel. Are you receiving me, Berlin. I repeat, cancel."

"It's too late. We can't stop them now. We'd have an incident if we fired." The driver was speaking urgently into the microphone.

Leipzig, Monday Night
In a call-box at the back of the hotel Miss Dixon had succeeded in putting a call through to London.

"It's me, Frances . . . No time for explanations now, Liz. I want you to go to Berlin. Here's the address . . . No. Straight away . . . What? Brander. I can explain all that. You don't know the background. I'll get a medal for it, I can tell you . . . No of course I'm all right. I wouldn't be phoning otherwise, would I? Look Liz, I tell you I want you straight away. Honestly I do. It's a great place for us, I can tell you . . . No. I can guarantee it. No trouble with the police. It was in the national interest, I can tell you . . . Good. I'll be waiting."

Miss Dixon stepped out of the box and looked at her watch. There wasn't much time.

TWENTY

Near Magdeburg, Monday Night

One of the contact men had produced a gun. Armstrong turned to face him.

"Where is the car to take us to Berlin?"

"There is no car. Stand, both of you together and raise your hands." One of the contact men was shouting at them in German. Jo looked across anxiously.

So this was it. There wasn't time to stop and consider whether they were going to shoot. Whether they were or not was irrelevant. The arrangements were being broken and it didn't look good.

"Flat on your face," Armstrong shouted at Jo. At the same time he kicked a spray of snow at the gunman's face. The man fired at him and missed. Armstrong seized a branch of wood which was lying on top of the snow, and swung it in a wild arc towards the man. He made contact for there was a howl of pain. The man had lost his gun. His partner, who had been standing a little away, ran up firing blindly. Then he stumbled and fell in the snow.

For a moment Armstrong thought Jo had disappeared, but she was there, kneeling, holding the first man's gun.

"I shot him." She almost sobbed as she spoke.

"Give me it." Armstrong snatched the gun from her. He turned to the two men, but there was little danger. One was lying quite still, where Jo had hit him. The other had taken to his heels. They could hear him crashing through the wood away from the road.

"He'll have reinforcements or a car in some side track that way," Armstrong said. The exit route to Magdeburg couldn't be far away.

"Leave him. Quick, the autobahn. The only chance is to try for a lift. Maybe we can wave down some Allied traffic—I doubt it, though. They are not allowed to stop. We mustn't get caught in the woods."

"Were they going to kill us?"

"I don't know. But something had gone wrong."

"But I must know. I've just shot someone."

"Come. Talk later. Run!"

They scrambled up over the deep ditch and over the metal crash-rail on to the autobahn. All the traffic seemed to be going the other way. The going was easier on the ice-covered tarmac.

"Watch. They drive fast. We'll get hit by a passing car most likely."

She came to a standstill and pulled at his arm. "Rest a moment. Let's think."

Armstrong stopped. She was right. He had been determined to get away from the immediate area. Now it was obvious to him that hitching a lift was a hopeless task. They would never stop a car from the West. No one was allowed to pick anyone up after dark, except the police. They would be on to them very quickly. The man who had run away would give the alarm.

They continued to walk along beside the autobahn. It would have been impossible to make any progress off the road. In the first five minutes only one car passed them. It was late, and the car was going very fast. The driver probably didn't even see them. Then they saw a lorry parked ahead. Its indicator light was flashing. That meant a breakdown.

"We'll try to get a lift. I'll reconnoitre first, just in case. If the driver doesn't look hopeful, we'll try a stowaway. Wait here." He gave her a quick hug of reassurance.

He saw the man with his head under the bonnet. Then he recognized the crates in the back. He almost shouted for joy.

"But I wasn't told about this. I have no papers for you."

We must empty some more crates."

"Too difficult. I have no tools with me."

"Then we'll come with you in the front. As we go, we can decide what to do."

"I was told it was all fixed." Günter Scholz was almost in tears.

"O.K., O.K. Relax. Have you found the fault?"

"Yes. I hadn't done up the wire securely enough after the last stop. It had got disconnected."

Armstrong and the girl squeezed into the cab. The engine started first time.

"I've lost some time. I have to be there by two o'clock precisely, that's what Hermes—Captain Hermes—said."

"You'll manage. Now what we'll do is this. Jo, you'll get in the back. We'll hope they won't search, since they're expecting the lorry through. We have to trust that this part of the deal, with the five in the back, was on the level. We also have to hope that we get to Helmstedt before the news gets through. They won't realize that we got on the same lorry, since the man who escaped will report that it had left before the fight. But they may try to hold up the deal in any case, until they catch us."

"And you?" Jo asked.

"I'm the co-driver, whether our friend here likes it or not. Remember, I have a gun now. . . . A last resort," he added, seeing Jo's look of concern.

"All right, stop just once more, driver. The lady is going in the back. No tricks now. I won't be a minute. I have to get her hidden, and tell the others what's going on."

Scholz pushed the papers across the counter towards the soldier. The wooden hut was just as he remembered it. It still stank of cigar smoke. He moved over to the wooden bench that lined the wall and settled down to wait. He had more of a grip now, though his heart was beating wildly. The man who was acting as co-driver needn't threaten. He would go through with it now. He remembered the man. He had interrogated him earlier.

The soldier called to him. Everything was in order. "Go out and clear yourself and cargo through control. Be good. The chief's on duty himself tonight," the soldier joked.

Scholz went out into the cold and walked slowly across to the cab.

"O.K.?" Armstrong asked.

"So far," Scholz grunted. He started the engine and drove across the cobbles towards the main, reinforced-concrete barrier. A soldier on duty called out that the check was at the last barrier. The chief was there.

They could see the final barrier ahead. A thin steel pole, painted red and white, showed up clearly against the snow. Beyond, they could see the lights of the Western checkpoint.

An officer came up to the lorry. He addressed Scholz. "What's the cargo?"

"Refrigerators, electric washing machines . . ."

The officer walked slowly to the front of the vehicle and looked at the registration plates. He checked the number against a document he held in his hand.

"Your name Scholz?"

"Yes."

"You were expected. But there is no word of a co-driver."

"There must be some mistake."

"Your papers?" The officer addressed Armstrong.

Scholz said "Weren't you told?" Armstrong thanked him inwardly. He had felt the driver might have weakened, but he was acting well.

"Yes, but there was no mention of a co-driver."

"There will be trouble . . ." Scholz almost began to enjoy himself. He had never talked to an officer like that before.

There was a shout. A soldier came running up to the officer shouting that the lorry must be stopped. The officer shouted back that he knew what he was doing. The soldier shrieked about a message. Everything had changed. The lorry must be stopped.

"Put your foot down." Armstrong needn't have

spoken. The lorry groaned forward. There was the sound of a shot and at the same instant the vehicle hit the barrier. There was a loud crash. The red and white pole was obviously stronger than it looked. The windscreen shattered but the lorry kept going. There were more sounds of firing. Ahead, Armstrong could see men in familiar khaki. They also had guns. But there was no firing. A soldier in a red Military Police cap came running up to the lorry.

"It's all right, Sergeant. I hope we're expected," Armstrong said.

East Berlin, Tuesday Evening

The little man sat cleaning his nails. The filings dropped as white dust on the table top.

They hadn't been angry. They never were. But he knew that they were displeased. In the old days his head would have fallen, metaphorically at least, but now were the days of collective authority, and generally speaking he could hide behind the decisions of committees and councils. Much more secure. But in this case there had been a large amount of personal responsibility involved, and he had been in charge of the execution of the operation. So there was the displeasure.

He thought of his opposite number. He had begun to think of Armstrong as his sparring partner ever since the meeting on the ice. The little man knew he might in other circumstances have been in Armstrong's shoes, not just a matter of changed roles—he might actually have had his job.

Oxford in the late thirties had been a great recruiting area for the world's spy-networks. Half-German with perfect English and a British passport, he had been a nåtural for the Nazi recruiting-officers to go after. He had played along for a while, but like so many of his contemporaries, he was no fascist, and he had enlisted secretly with the communist opposition to Hitler, while continuing to play along with Hitler's man.

Later, since Russia was so far away, he had joined the ranks of the British espionage net, in an attempt to bring his country back to sanity. He wondered if Armstrong knew that—he would have approved his background so far. It was only after the war that he had seen his political convictions pull him into the service of the other Germany. He had had his regrets. He liked the comfortable life and the more democratic way the British had of doing things. If he had stayed, he might indeed . . .

He put the nail-file carefully in its case and returned it to his pocket. Then he blew away the dust from the table top, stood up and walked to the window. It was snowing again. He thought of Miss Dixon. He didn't trust her, but they did. He could smell a triple agent a mile away. Once one had been acting for two sides, it was easy to slip back yet again. He had seen it happen before.

He made a slight face. Perhaps he was being too suspicious, and letting his natural dislike of women, in particular this peculiar one, to carry away his reason. But it would be easy to check. This time nothing had to go wrong. He looked at his nails thoughtfully.

TWENTY-ONE

West Berlin, Thursday Evening

The meeting was obviously well under way when they arrived, and they slipped unobtrusively into an empty row of seats at the back of the room.

The hall was large and cold, built in prewar institutional style, and not apparently decorated since. Above the platform, a large black and gold banner proclaimed unity and peace. Behind it could be seen the remains of some more permanent emblazonment dating from the hall's National Socialist past.

The speaker was a man in his middle fifties. He was hammering theatrically at the table in front of him, his words giving the lie at least in part to the motto on the banner above him. It was apparently only by immediate and, if necessary, violent action, against neo-fascist capitalism, that the political goals could be achieved. Some comrades, including the two other members of the platform party who were both half the speaker's age, vigorously applauded the sentiment.

The audience was also mostly young; beards and Mao-type tunics were common. Students for the most part, come from the Free University for the meeting. There was a sprinkling of older people, workers and hard-faced men perhaps over from the other side for the evening, to give body to the occasion. Everyone listened attentively. It was a very serious political gathering.

Armstrong had had the message from London. Miss Dixon had been in touch again. She had confirmed they were dead. Perhaps she hadn't been told. She said she was intent on getting back now that it was all over. It might be difficult but she thought she could manage to arrange to be at the meeting with a group of comrades who would be there to "protect" her. She had persuaded them to let her over to collect additional intelligence material from a contact who would only hand the stuff to her. Could the organization be there to pick her up and give her safe passage? It mustn't be too obvious or they might suspect.

The story was thin, but there was just a chance she might come.

The speaker was on to Vietnam. The audience applauded every sentence.

"No sign yet," Jo whispered, touching Armstrong's sleeve.

"Keep the collar of your coat up. There's plenty of time." Armstrong was watching a man by the door, one of Hermes' men who was to tip him off if someone answering Miss Dixon's description appeared. Others were placed outside. It had been carefully planned and Armstrong had decided to go along himself and take Jo with him. There was little risk, and they were the only two in Berlin who could recognize her. Thereafter, everything was fixed; a special flight to take her back, and from Berlin one didn't even need an extradition warrant.

One speaker finished. A younger man took his place.

A generation of difference, but the slogans and the catch-words were the same. Armstrong looked at his watch and yawned.

Half an hour went by. Again he looked at his watch. She might have discovered the truth by now. Then what would she do? She couldn't risk a come-back if he was still about. And the little man had nothing to gain by keeping her in the dark. So was it a trap? It seemed so far-fetched, and it was pointless to speculate. But they had taken every precaution. All he knew was that he shared the organization's desire to get her back. They had no need to urge him to pull out all the stops. He was personally involved.

A crowd of men came into the room. Something was slightly odd about them. Armstrong suddenly realized why. They all looked so alike. They all were dressed in very much the same way, fairly neatly, suits and ties, which showed up against the dress of the rest of the audience.

There were about fifteen in all. They stood in the door-way, and none of them made any attempt to sit down, though there were plenty of empty chairs. They waited as if for a signal. Jo looked enquiringly across at Armstrong. He shrugged.

The signal came. The speaker mentioned fascist control of the press or some such thing, and immediately a barrage of heckling came from the group in the door-way. Not simple political heckling, but well-organized continuous shouting of abuse which forced the speaker to abandon his speech. Counter-heckling followed from the rest of the audience. People stood up and the two rival groups started to square up to each other. A chair was thrown. Someone punched someone. There was fire or was it a smoke bomb? In seconds it was like a battle-field.

"The Nationalists. They come from time to time to break up such meetings. It keeps their hands in. I've read about it," Jo shouted across the din.

"Well, let's get out. I don't fancy a chair across the head at this juncture. We can watch for her outside."

It was easier said than done. The entrance was blocked by fighting men. Then they saw the little door by the side of the platform. It was slightly open, and framed in the doorway stood Miss Dixon. Just for a moment, then she saw them and was gone. The door banged shut.

They ran over to it. "There's a danger that she may have a weapon." Armstrong had produced a revolver. "Keep well back. She'll have a hard time getting out the back way. They'll pick her up." He looked round the hall for reinforcements, but none of Hermes' men were visible.

"I'm going to drive her out. You stay here," Armstrong said. Jo ignored the order and kept closely behind him as they pushed their way together into a dimly lit passageway that smelt of drains. There was no sign of Miss Dixon. Ahead of them were two further doors. Armstrong pushed against one marked "Exit" but it refused to open.

"This must lead to fresh air," Armstrong said.

"You're quite right, Armstrong, it does. Raise your hands, both of you." The little man had appeared from an alcove behind them. There were three men with him.

M

"That revolver, if you please, and I have Miss Weinberg on target. Quickly now, no fooling. We don't want your friends to arrive just yet."

One of the men took the gun. Another had produced a key from his pocket and unlocked the other door.

"Through. Quickly!"

"You realize we have this place surrounded." Armstrong regained his composure somewhat.

"We'll see. Through you go." They went into what appeared to be a small dressing-room.

"One word and I'll shoot. I assure you of that, Armstrong. And just to cheer you up, remember my friends and I are on home ground so to speak. We chose the pitch, and Captain Hermes, who, I imagine, is outside somewhere helping to control the 'riot' we arranged, may not have studied the layout of this place as well as he might."

"We have every exit covered."

The little man didn't reply. Already one of the others was down on his knees on the floor. He had a screwdriver in his hand. A trapdoor opened, and a chill rush of air entered the room. Armstrong felt his control slipping.

The cellar room was cold and wet. They had to stand since there was nothing they could find to sit on. The walls were slimy to the touch, and parts of the uneven floor were covered in water. Cobwebs coated their faces. It was pitch dark.

"I imagine they're leaving us here till the hunt for us dies down. They won't risk moving us till then. After that . . . well, I imagine they haven't gone to all this trouble just to bump us off. I should think they'll try to get us over to the other side again."

"But why should they want us?" Jo asked.

"Revenge, interrogation . . . I don't know. It doesn't matter. It was a well-organized trap anyway. It's always easiest to catch someone just after a crisis. He thinks he's won through and he's off guard."

"And the Nationalists?"

"Could be a put-up job. Could be real. In any case it served their purpose. I suppose they knew I was in Berlin and would be bound to spring at the bait. It's all obvious now. Miss Dixon . . . my, what a morsel." Armstrong laughed thinly. Then he reached out and grasped her hand. It was cold.

"Lean against the wall, at least. It's foul, but we have to try to conserve our strength." He put his arm round her.

Three or four hours, he guessed. They had taken their watches. His feet were frozen and sodden. They both stiffened as they heard the sound at the old iron door. A light streamed in, temporarily blinding them. The little man stood in the doorway.

"Sorry about the accommodation. But you realize the difficulty. Your people took a long time to leave. Eventually we managed to provide a 'witness' to say you had left."

They stumbled out into the light. The same three men who had been with him before were there. They were all armed. Miss Dixon was nowhere to be seen. They were led along a stone corridor.

"It leads to an old air-raid shelter," the little man explained helpfully. "There are a lot of them still about. Quite a warren in some places. You'll see."

Up some rusty iron stairs, and into the back premises of some shop. Out of the single window of the room, Armstrong saw the meeting hall across the road. Obviously the two premises had shared the shelter.

A black van with a driver was waiting outside. At gun point they were made to get in the back with two of the men. There were no windows, so that they had no idea of where they were being driven. Twenty minutes had gone by, Armstrong guessed, when they came to a stop.

The house was of the same type as the one in Charlottenburg. Berlin seemed to be full of them. The street was deserted. Suddenly Armstrong knew why. At one end, the street suddenly stopped. There was the Wall. Old tram lines ran down the centre of the street and under the Wall. They probably continued on the other side.

They went towards the house. The door was opened by a man in a leather coat who stood aside as they came into the bare hall. As the door shut behind them, Armstrong heard the van drive away. So wherever they were going it wasn't by road.

"Where is Miss Dixon—the grey-haired English woman?" Armstrong heard the little man ask the leather-coated janitor in German.

"But she was to come with you."

"There'll be trouble if she's been caught. You were to stick with her."

"But you said she knew. She was to be trusted. She said she would manage on her own. . . ."

"She said what? All right. Never mind now. Which way?" The little man shrugged and seemed to forget Miss Dixon.

"Down these stairs, and then to the left. The passage goes fifty metres or so, then there is a wall. The Allies made it a year or two back. You'll see the wire to the left. Three pulls. Quite simple. They have the wall all ready at the other side. No, it's O.K. We've used it before. I cement it from this side once you're through. No one expects traffic the other way."

All so simple. Armstrong looked across at Jo. She had understood, too. This was it.

"You'll have to wait half an hour. They aren't at the other side yet." The man in the leather coat looked at his watch. Half an hour. It wasn't long.

"I'm sure she'll turn up in time." Armstrong addressed the little man with a smile.

"What do you mean?" The little man looked sharply at him.

"I'm sure Miss Dixon's just got lost. Her friend, of course . . ."

"I don't know what game you're playing, Armstrong. But I'm not interested. Be quiet, or I'll have to shut you up until we go over. You've caused enough trouble. One of my best men died by the autobahn."

"You should have kept your word."

"I promised nothing."

"You gave me to understand."

"We're not playing cricket, Armstrong."

"Exactly." Armstrong again remarked the little man's perfect command of English. Where had he been educated? "Exactly. And if one side breaks the rules, then the game doesn't stop. The other side breaks the rules too, and the game goes on."

"It's nearly over."

"We'll see. But, tell me, why do you want us? Is it to stand trial for having helped your colleague on his way?"

"Oh, you won't come to trial. No. They want you all. And Miss Dixon. I don't understand. It's not quite my field, but they have methods now of getting co-operation from unwilling . . . subjects, and our mission is to get you to help do what your Minister began. The erosion of your organization must be allowed to continue."

"Are you putting out that I defected?"

"Perhaps. It's quite a good idea, isn't it? Then after a course of treatment you may be released again."

Brain-washing and reinfiltration. Surely not. It was too obvious. But it had happened before. And this time they had Miss Dixon to help things along. Perhaps that was meant to have been Alex's fate. . . .

"As I said, of course," Armstrong smiled, "Miss Dixon will probably turn up."

The little man pretended not to notice, but Armstrong knew he had him hooked. He went on: "She's coming with us, I presume? If you're looking for her she's sure to be with her friend saying goodbye. After all the girl—Liz—was coming out from London specially to see her. You knew that, didn't you? A long way to come just for an hour. Seems it might be more permanent, don't you think?"

"You don't know anything about a friend."

"Oh, I don't *know* her friend, Liz. Miss Dixon's taste in friendships is not mine. I think you know what I mean. . . ." Armstrong felt he had gone far enough. He mustn't overdo it. Just enough of a hint that Miss Dixon wasn't acting according to pattern. It might just help. It did.

The little man didn't seem to need much convincing. He turned to the man in the leather coat again. "How long have we still got?"

"Twenty-five minutes, about. Otherwise we have to wait twenty-four hours. They can't man it all the time. Too risky."

"Right. You're in charge here. I'll be back in twenty minutes. Don't let them out of your sight. They've escaped once before, and killed someone in the process. You're warned. Where do I find a car? I have to pick someone up."

The twenty minutes seemed like hours. They hadn't been given their watches back. They weren't allowed to speak to each other, nor even to sit down on the filthy floor. Jo leant exhaustedly against the peeling wall. The man in the leather coat and the other guards watched them like hawks.

After a while the leather-coated man began to show his anxiety and kept looking at his watch. Armstrong realized that the time must almost be up. Then they might gain twenty-four hours. A lot could happen in that time.

There was a noise at the door. It opened, and the little man came into the room.

"We go without her," he said simply.

"So I was right," Armstrong remarked.

"Shut up. Let's go." The leather-coated man went forward and opened the cellar door.

Armstrong decided there was nothing to lose by keeping talking. "So she has given you the slip. I expected it. I must . . ."

"Shut up, I said." The little man was sweating. He had obviously been running.

"She wants to make a come-back this side, hedging her bets again. Did your superiors really think she was being level with you? You at least must have guessed."

The little man swung round. "For the last time, Armstrong . . . You might provoke me too far."

"I'd call that the failure of a mission. . . ." As Armstrong began again, the leather-coated man stuck a gun hard in his ribs, and forced him to the door. Jo was made to go first, finding her way down worn steps with the dim light from a torch. She almost slipped in the dark and hesitated, but a guard pushed her on roughly. At the bottom the going was easier, though the floor was rough. The little man produced a second torch. They walked about fifty metres, and there was the wall. The leather-coated man pulled the wire, slowly, three times. Almost immediately, the centre bricks in the wall started moving as somebody started working through from the other side. It was a weird experience.

The first brick disappeared showing a pair of hands in a patch of light. Then another brick. In a few minutes there was a hole big enough for someone to squeeze through.

A face appeared. Another man in a leather coat.

"All O.K.?" he asked in German.

"Almost," the little man replied.

"Aren't there two women?"

"That's the almost, Lieutenant. But let's get on with it. You go first." The little man turned to Jo.

Jo didn't move, and the leather-coated man seized her by the arm. As he did so, he seemed to crumple up beside her. The noise of the gunshot was unbearable in the confined space. It happened again. The face in the hole disappeared. One of the other guards seemed to fall. The noise came from behind. Armstrong was flat on the floor. Jo was lying behind the leather coat. A flash and a third roar came from the passage they had just walked along. Armstrong felt a pain in his right leg. He couldn't move his body, but when he turned his head, he was aware of a pair of legs sticking out of the hole in the wall. They wriggled, and the little man disappeared from view. That would spoil his suit and manicure, Armstrong thought. He began to laugh, as Tesco appeared from the darkness.

"I followed Miss Dixon after the riot. By pure chance I saw her leave. Some lout had just broken my camera with a chair, and I was trying to pick up the bits. She ran past me. I followed. A bit later I saw that I wasn't alone. The little man was watching her too. But she gave us both the slip, so I followed the little man instead."

Tesco sat back contentedly in a deep chair, plump hands round a whisky glass. Armstrong groaned as a nurse bandaged his leg. The masonry dislodged by one of the bullets had made a nasty mess of his knee. Jo had a towel and was mopping his forehead. Some girl of Hermes' was taking it all down in shorthand. Quite pretty looking, but a bit hard-bitten. Armstrong looked up at Jo and smiled. Funny, he felt quite light-headed. He giggled slightly.

Tesco stood up and poured out another whisky and handed it to Armstrong. "Relax," he said. "I'll carry on when you're feeling better."

Armstrong frowned. Better? He was fine, apart from the knee, wasn't he? He appealed to the nurse. She was agreeing as he passed out.

TWENTY-TWO

West Berlin, Friday Night

The elderly prostitute stood in the deep shadow by a shop window at the south-east end of Augustusstrasse. It was late. She'd be in luck if she caught anyone. She always felt lucky now when she caught anyone. This would be the last winter on the beat. Then off to the Black Forest and her little house there.

She nodded at a passing policeman. They were good men most of them. They left her alone, respecting her age perhaps. She hadn't been pulled in for years now. She was an institution.

A little man came along the street towards her. She pulled back into the darkness. With luck she could get him back to the seedy hotel before he realized her age. The room she had was dark. If he was a bit drunk . . .

There was this big woman on the other side of the street as well. Not one of the girls, yet it was unusual to see a lone woman in Augustusstrasse at that time of night. It was a woman, wasn't it? Pretty masculine looking. Perhaps it was one of them. She seemed a bit nervous, kept looking over her shoulder.

The prostitute gave a short gasp. The little man was right up beside her, and she hadn't noticed.

"Like a good time, dearie?"

He came up to her. Instinctively she reached in her

bag for the little pepper cannister she carried in case of emergencies.

"No," he whispered back. "But it's worth fifty marks if you walk with me for the next minute or two. See that woman over there?"

"Yes. You a policeman or something?"

"Private investigator. But don't you worry. Just divorce action enquiries. Let's go. We have to keep her in view," he whispered.

"Judging from her looks it would be a lucky husband who got rid of her."

"O.K., let's have less chatter." He seemed abrupt and nervous. Funny chap, pretty feminine looking. She walked beside him in silence for a moment.

"As this is a strange thing, can I see the colour of your money, dearie. I have my rent to think of."

He handed her a fifty mark note without stopping. The other woman was perhaps fifty yards in front of them. She paused and looked back. The little man turned to his companion and to her surprise put his arms round her.

"Let's act the part then," he said. The prostitute felt him wince as he came in contact with her.

"You do rush a girl so," she joked. Then she saw the look in his eyes and stopped.

"I'm not having more of this. Here's your fifty back. You're up to no good." She thrust the note at the man.

He smiled, attempting to reassure her.

"Don't worry," he said, "I'm just trying to earn my keep, same as you. There'll be another fifty for you at the end if you stay with me. It shouldn't be long."

She was mollified and the money would help.

"O.K., O.K. But keep your distance. I don't often say that to men, but . . ."

The woman ahead of them was walking quickly again. They followed after. She turned left into a side street, and by the time they had reached the corner, she was turning into a brightly lit door.

"So she is one of them. That's what I thought," the prostitute muttered.

"What's that place?"

"Don't you know? It's well known to the tourists. All women together. Disgusting, I call it."

"Here's your other fifty."

"Are you finished with me, then?"

"Yes, and forget you ever saw me."

She took the money. "Glad to do that I'm sure." She waddled away into the darkness.

The little man was desperately tired. Denied all sleep since the plan had misfired, now like a shuttle-cock, he was back in the Western Sector once again. He had started to argue that it hadn't been him who had trusted Miss Dixon, but Authority had been stonily unabashed. "Tidy things up immediately," was how they had phrased it, as they slipped him through yet another tear in the very tattered Curtain.

Liz was drunk and a little hysterical. Miss Dixon looked at her severely. She had got out of hand a bit while she had been away. A little discipline would do Liz good.

They sat together on a velvet couch watching the

floor-show. It was of a good standard. Even not speaking German, she got most of the patter. The girls were good. She'd have to come here a bit more often. One of them really was . . . Yes, she had to admit it, she was a bit bored with Liz.

The club was hung with mock Victorian hangings. The place looked as if it needed a good cleaning. The bottle of *Sekt* in front of them was good though, and at the price, it should have been. Around the walls were prints of hunting scenes with peculiar modern overtones. Almost pornographic, some of them. The other guests were amiable enough, except for a couple of rather embarrassed heterosexual American tourists.

"I feel sick," Liz announced. "It's that b-bubbly." She rose unsteadily and advanced towards the door marked "ladies and gentlemen".

Miss Dixon sighed, and turned her attentions to one of the girl performers who was now giggling beside her. It was only when the latter rose to perform her act again, that Miss Dixon realized that Liz had not returned.

"Stupid girl," she thought. "I must take her home and knock some sense into her." She took a little sip from her glass of *Sekt*, stood up and walked towards the door through which Liz had disappeared.

The elderly prostitute saw the three cars arrive and pull up outside the brightly lit door. A police raid, she thought. But as far as she could see it was none of the usual men. Over the years she had got to know most of the city's Vice Squad pretty well. If they were new, she'd better get out of the road. She couldn't afford to be pulled in just now. Apart from the hundred marks in her pocket, things were pretty hard. She smiled to herself as she scuttled away. That club had had it coming to it. Bad for her trade, that sort of perversion.

"Looks as if it was done with a long thin knife." Hermes was talking. They all looked down at the huddled bundle on the floor. Outside the small room they could hear the raised voices and shouts as the police cleared the club. On a chair in the corner, a policeman helped by Jo was removing the adhesive tape from the legs, wrists and mouth of an hysterical Liz.

"It could have been a nail-file," Armstrong suggested. The police Captain shrugged indifferently.

"Well, a story at last," Tesco looked happy. He took out a note pad, and began unstrapping his new camera.

The men and the girl stared at him. Tesco suddenly realized he was the centre of attention.

"I have *got* a story?" he asked, almost pleading.

Armstrong shook his head slowly.

West Berlin, Friday Night
At high noon on the brightest of days, Frankenstrasse is a grim street. On one side, shabby tenements, on the other, the Wall, a weird jigsaw of breeze-blocks and the shells of former houses locked together in demented embrace. There is no attempt at compromise or disguise. A faded wooden sign left untouched above a walled-up door, still invites customers to have their shoes inexpensively mended within. Further on, the grey Wall

cuts a precise diagonal among the greyer stones of an unattended graveyard.

In Frankenstrasse, at quarter past one in the morning, the sodium floodlights on their almost graceful curved columns, blend with the falling snow and mellow the harshness of the scene. The little man's elegant shoes are paper thin, and the slush soaks quickly through to his silk socks. He hurries. He is already very late and they dislike to be kept waiting when it is a matter of opening up the Wall.

He pauses briefly, bends forward, and a steel sliver of evidence disappears down a drain by the road side. He looks at his watch for the tenth time, then hesitantly pulls into a doorway to recover his breath.

For perhaps twenty seconds he allows a prospect of self-preservation to take over from deep-seated discipline. He sees comfort and welcome in the West; on the other side, the consequences of a failed mission.

For these few seconds rationality wins. Then, closing his mind abruptly, the little man walks on quickly down the street.